THE LOP-SIDED MAN

JACOB ELLIOTT

ISBN: 979-8-9905910-0-4 (paperback)

ISBN: 979-8-9905910-1-1 (ebook)

Edited by Mark Becker

Cover art by Ed Wishewsky

For Mom and Dad, who did a much better job of raising me than the contents of this book may suggest.

AUGUST

1

The horror started, as most things of a certain nature do, in the dead of night. Nathan had just tucked his boy into bed and poured himself a strong glass of whiskey over ice. He stood above the kitchen sink and took a sip. He pursed his lips for a single second. The liquid burned going down and left behind a hollow feeling of being cleansed deep in his stomach. He took another sip, and his lips didn't purse at all. He took a third, and the burning stopped. It used to take him a full drink to reach this point. Now, he was down to just three sips.

How's that for progress, Landry...

Landry was Nathan's therapist. He started seeing her as soon as his wife left him. Well—was she the one who left him? On paper, she was the one who filed for divorce, so he supposed she got to wear that badge. But it had been his fault in the end. Hard for a woman to stay with a man after he admits that he's been gay through the eight years of their relationship —five of which involved marriage and a kid who, despite his interest pointing otherwise, was indeed biologically his. So, he supposed in a way, he left Hollie long before she was ever interested in leaving him.

He didn't cheat on her or anything like that. He wouldn't dare do something so dark-hearted, so gnarled and nasty. Hollie Smart was a kind woman who he had certifiably and undeniably fallen in love with. They met in college, as many young couples do, and started as friends in their Fairytales class, an elective designed to explore the reality behind the childlike tales and find the deeper meanings scattered throughout them. Nathan had always loved fairytales, and not in the Disney coded way where he wanted a prince and a princess to kiss and fall in love and right the wrongs in the world. He liked them for the secrets they kept. Little Red's loss of innocence to the Big Bad Wolf. Rapunzel's reality of daily assault while she slept, unable to fend off her attacker.

Nathan sat with Hollie as her own version of a romantic's perfect fairytale came crashing down. Her first major breakup happened a year into their friendship, and he held her while she cried that night. He told her he loved what she was and what she saw when she looked at the world. Told her he envied her because he did. Her rosy gaze seemed preferable to the harsh lines and grey tones that painted his reality. And somewhere in all of that, she kissed him. In hindsight, he thought maybe he knew it even then—that he was gay—but he had never been with a man, or a girl for that matter, and the whole moment had felt so...*right*. Like one of those fairytale moments brought briefly to life.

So, they got together. Part rebound, part desperate plea for normalcy, though none of that mattered. They were together at twenty and they stayed that way as the years went by. And, all things considered, he was happy. He didn't question whether it was right because, *of course*, being with Hollie Smart never felt wrong. It never felt wrong in bed as he slid inside her and had to contain the full body shivers she gave him every time. It never felt wrong as they kissed while they strode through campus hand in hand, laughing about whatever someone had said or someone else had done. It never felt wrong because it never *was* wrong.

Until suddenly, *everything* was.

Now, as he poured his drink and let it slowly take effect, Nathan credited the stopping to that stupid soap Hollie had been watching. She always had it on in the background as they cooked dinner or while Nathan worked. He was an aspiring writer with a bad habit of handwriting all his work, only to get frustrated and throw it in the fire or tear it in half whenever something didn't work. "I'll keep it together when it's right," he told Hollie one night when she threw a fit at his flame stoking creativity. "If it's wrong, it's just wrong. Simple as that."

Well, that soap was on; an old show from the 70s or so. If there was a plot, Nathan could never pinpoint it. He hardly paid attention most of the time. At best, he glanced up when someone was screwing someone else or shouting in an aggressive manner. That night, he looked up as one of the main love interests was in the shower. Soapy suds dripped down his built chest and impressive torso. The camera panned lower and lower until suddenly cutting to black with the sound of shattering glass. Hollie gasped audibly. Nathan turned to her, then, when she turned his way, he quickly looked down at the chicken scratch covered paper across his lap. He felt her gaze on him even as he continued writing. Or pretended to write, rather. His mind was still on the show, and it would remain that way until the next morning when Hollie left for a weekend trip away with the girls.

That night, he thought again about the show; this time while water ran down his own torso and steam billowed up around his feet. It was customary that he take a longer shower whenever Hollie wasn't around. It eased his mind, released the tension in his muscles. Tonight, it did something more. His hand traveled down his own pudgy stomach until he was gripping his own cock and, well—the rest came quite naturally. So naturally, in fact, that it took all but two minutes to finish and wash away any remains of the dirty deed. He stood under the shower head after that for some time. His mind was suddenly racing. That had been quicker than he ever remembered with Hollie. *You savor it when it's with someone,* he thought. Because sure, sure you did. But he hadn't been savoring it the last few times when neither of them had finished. He'd gone limp before they could. And while he had done what he could to help her get to the finish line, his heart just hadn't been in it.

He turned off the water and let his body drip dry before reaching for the black towel hanging over the shower door. He opened the shower and stepped into the bathroom. The mirror was steamy, and his face was invisible behind the smog. How long had he been in there?

Two minutes, he thought. *Just two minutes for—*

He threw the towel over his head and rubbed it frantically against his skull. His hair came up looking wild when he pulled the towel off but he didn't care. He hardly saw himself in the slowly clearing glass.

He still saw that man from the soap opera. That man whose body was better than his and whose chest was full and arms were wide.

Nathan figured he was jealous of the man's physique and swore to get back to the gym. He hadn't been going since starting a new job the year prior, and it was starting to show. He'd always been slim, but lately his stomach jutted out a bit and his slender arms were a bit fuller without the definition a workout routine would provide.

Yeah, yeah I'm just jealous.

And maybe he was. But a month later, when Hollie wasn't around, he did the same thing. This time it took longer than two minutes and his other hand wrapped around and grabbed his ass in a way Hollie never did. It felt quite nice, and he finished shortly after. He wondered briefly what else might feel nice against his ass.

Later that night, he brought the topic to Hollie. She could grab him there the next time they were...

"Oh, I don't know if I'm into all that, Nate," she said. Then, seeing the steely shock on his face, she said, "But we can try it!"

When they did, it didn't feel the same as he thought, and he informed her shortly after that they didn't need to try that one again. She was clearly thankful and never mentioned it after that night. Slowly, the two stopped making love. Nathan masturbated more frequently—sometimes even while Hollie was home, and usually while they could have instead been doing it together—and every time he was picturing things he shouldn't have been. He was married, and in love. What was he doing picturing a man on his knees before him in the shower, or a man standing behind him and pushing him against the tile? Always in the shower. Always against the sharp, cold tiles with a mountain of slippery soap sudsing up his body.

He did get back to the gym, though. He found it

was one of the few things that took his mind off the inevitable. Pretty soon he was back to being toned, and—if Hollie was to be believed—his arms were looking "pretty damn sexy lately..." She made eyes at him the night she said it and he could tell she was in a mood. He was too, but not the kind of mood that involved her. It involved him, their shower, and an imagination full of scenarios he refused to let play out. But he decided that wasn't practical. He couldn't avoid fucking his wife for the rest of their lives. Especially because, at the end of the day, he liked it. She knew what she was doing; she knew his body and what felt good, and she knew how to at least act like he knew the same for her. So, he decided, tonight was the night. He would throw caution to the wind and fuck her like he had when they first got together. That was all he needed, really. Sometimes a good fucking could knock the sense right into you.

He drank his first whiskey over ice that night. With a tipsy mind and blurry vision, he took Hollie to their bed and made love to her. It felt good that night, better than it had in ages. They spent hours tossing each other back and forth. He pushed her head down toward his cock. She lowered his between her legs. He fingered her; she grabbed his ass without him having to ask, and eventually, after hours of foreplay, he entered her. He came almost instantly after that, and she did the same. They collapsed beside one another, out of breath and drenched in sweat, and decided a shower was in order.

When they got to the shower, he fucked her again. He took her in ways he'd only ever imagined, and with each raging thrust, he threw out the idea of whatever had overcome him the last few months. This was who he was, this was what he was meant to be doing, and no men on tv or at the gym could come between that.

He thought about those men as he pushed in for the final thrust.

Two weeks later, Hollie told him she was pregnant.

He didn't really know what that would mean for him until Tyler was born. Other than helping more around the house and picking up more groceries than he was used to—Hollie was "eating for two" and she made sure that everyone around her knew it—his life stayed about the same. He drank more frequently, but never touched the whiskey bottle he'd opened the night Tyler was conceived. If it brought about kids, he was better off keeping that one on the tip-top shelf and forgetting about it for a while.

After Tyler was born, he realized how much more complicated everything had suddenly become.

In the nine months it took from the day Hollie missed her period to the day she was in the hospital bed, popping a baby boy out headfirst, Nathan's urges hadn't gone away. He kept them tepid by masturbating once a week. That was his rule to himself. Every Sunday night before the work week started again, he got in the shower and relieved himself. He didn't think about Hollie or their unborn son or how his life was about to change. He thought about the guy who had been lifting a few stations over from him, or the new guy at work who had a particular sway in his hips as he walked down the aisle of cubicles in dress slacks that seemed to be a size or two too small. He imagined what it would be like to pull him into an empty conference room, talk to him about those pants, tell him he would need to remove them or risk getting fired and, well...take it from there. He looked forward to

Sundays because Sundays felt like a treat after a long, hard week of...

A long hard week of *what*, exactly?

When Tyler was born, his Sunday nights vanished. Suddenly, there was a baby in the mix. A crying, snotty, red-faced baby who seemed to always be pouting or spitting up or needing something that he couldn't quite explain to either of his parents. Always...except for when Nathan tucked him into bed. It was early on that Hollie and Nathan discovered that *he* was the secret to getting their perpetual crier to calm down at a reasonable hour and sleep through a majority of the night.

"I don't do anything special."

"Doesn't matter—whatever you're doing, it works, so just..." If he wasn't mistaken, there was something almost crestfallen about the way Hollie spoke, "keep doing it."

She walked away after that. Discussion over. And Nathan had a new nighttime routine. No more showers and imaginary hookups with men he shouldn't be looking twice at. Now, he spent his Sundays staring down at a crib that looked like a crypt, with a wriggling baby staring up at him. The first time he did it, the boy's eyes had filled with a strange kind of wonder only present in the young. He tilted his head, and Tyler tilted his back. He tilted it the other way; Tyler followed. Nathan's lips spread into a grin, and Tyler started to laugh. He squinted his eyes, and his rosy cheeks grew somehow rounder. Nathan let out a breath and reached into the crib. He cradled Tyler, and he started to tell him a fairytale.

He told him stories for the next nine months. In a way, it was his turn to carry the child he had a hand in creating. Hollie stayed home for those months, first on maternity leave, then she used her remaining PTO, and finally left her job at the local art museum to be a stay-at-home mother. Nathan made enough money for the both of them, so he was fine with it. Besides, when he got home from work, Hollie was always ready for a break, and he was always ready to pick Tyler up, place him on his bouncing knee, and talk to him. And oh, they talked about everything. Colors and shapes and fairytales and stories. And life. They talked about life, too. How sometimes it got hard to be truthful when you were staring back at yourself in the mirror.

Tyler was just ten months old when Nathan told him he thought he was gay. He said it like that too. "I think...I mean...nobody can ever really be sure, right? You see, I love your mom. With all my heart, big fella, I swear it, I do. But sometimes I just...sometimes I just wonder..." He carried on like that for God knows how long, sputtering and stumbling out sentences that didn't connect or string together to form any kind of sentence with merit, until finally he bowed his head in the dim light of the single crib-side lamp in Tyler's room and said, "I think I'm gay, bud."

Tyler's laughing went silent then, and Nathan felt his heartstrings go taut. "It's just a thought," he said, not sure why he was justifying himself to a newborn.

FWOOMP!

The door slammed shut. Nathan turned and Tyler shifted in his arms. The door to the nursery stood there, open moments before and now closed, like a barrier between Nathan and his boy, and the outside world.

And Hollie.

Hollie!

No, no, no, no—

He stood up frantically and set Tyler back in his

crib. He started to cry as soon as his rump touched the soft blanket. Nathan looked back once, tried to smile at him to alleviate the sound, but he couldn't do it. Tyler sobbed harder when he saw the look in Nathan's eyes. Nathan winced.

"Everything's fine," he said aloud.

Tyler sniffled again and fell onto his back. Should Nathan be worried about him rolling over? Babies did that, right? They asphyxiated on the spot or something like that? He took a half step toward the crib, then heard another door slam. The bedroom door. He turned on his heels and ran for the door. He threw it open and shouted into the darkened hallway, "Hollie!"

He didn't wait for her response. He raced down the hall like a fighter jet. When he reached the closed door of the master bedroom, half of him expected it would be locked. But they had never been the kind of couple to get mad and lock one another out. Hell, they hardly ever got mad at one another. *She's my best friend* —But best friend only went so far when you were meant to want to grab your best friend, throw them against the bed, and have your way with them.

Which I've done before...

Not since Tyler though; no...not since Tyler.

He pulled open the door and felt a cold rush of bedtime air. *"You feel that breeze?" he told Tyler once. "That's the bedtime breeze. It's colder, so you've gotta wrap yourself up in your blankets like this—" He grabbed one corner of the yellow blanket under Tyler's wriggling body and folded it over the baby. "And thiiis." He grabbed the other. Tyler was laughing and looking up at him, and despite the bedtime breeze, Nathan felt warm. He finished wrapping up his baby burrito and picked Tyler up, held him in his arms, and swayed back and forth. "And now the bedtime breeze can't getcha...it can't getcha...it can't getcha... He looked over and saw Hollie standing in the open doorway and smiling. Her shoulder was against the door and her arms were crossed. "You two are ridiculous," she said through a budding laugh. "Oh please," he said back to her. "If you could stop the bedtime breeze from gettin' ya, you would too!" And then he walked toward her, and they both laughed with a giggling Tyler between them.*

Hollie had her back turned to him as he entered. The bedtime breeze cut sharp against his bare sleeves, and he noticed her arms were crossed. The curtains were drawn shut but billowed from the open window behind them. They always kept it open during summer nights. It was just about the only time they could guarantee the humidity was down long enough to cool the place. Summers in Michigan were gorgeous. Bright days on the lake, sunny picnics in the park with either boba tea or fresh smoothies...but summers in Michigan were also killer, especially when you couldn't fall asleep without the room at a certain temperature. They needed fresh air at night. The bedtime breeze. In his mind, he could practically hear the sharp metallic *scriiiish* of her drawing the curtains closed only seconds before. She stared past them, as if seeing the window beyond. Her shoulders were squared.

"Hollie—" He reached over and set a hand on each shoulder. She tensed under his touch. He lifted his hands.

"Just...Give me a minute," she said. "Please.

"I..." He took a step back. "I don't know what you heard."

She shook her head and turned to face him. "Neither do I. Would you..." She trailed off, lowered her head, and let out a breath. Nathan cracked one of his knuckles. "No," she suddenly said. "No, no, I don't want to hear it. I don't know what I heard, and I don't want to think about it."

"That's fine. We don't have to." *We don't have to think about sexuality or labels or all the mistakes we've made. We can just climb into bed, darling. Here, let me get the covers for you. Let's be normal for a bit. I'll grab you by the waist and pull you closer. You'll try to pull away but secretly want it, too. Then we'll fuck. Because we're married and I love you and I love fucking you. We both love fucking. We have to. We made a kid after all. And he's an amazing and special little boy. See, Darling we're normal. Absolutely norm—*

"No," she stopped him. "No, we *do* have to. Just... not now."

And then she collapsed. Her body keeled forward; her knees buckled beneath her. Nathan grabbed at her falling body and hefted her up before she could hit the ground. She let out a moaning wail that contorted her face into something unrecognizable. Then another—And another—

"Babe, babe, it's okay. It's—"

"Don't call me that! Stop it!"

He stopped breathing for a second, and there was a sudden silence around the room. He let Hollie fall the rest of the way to the floor and stepped back. She stopped heaving and just kept her head down. Her eyes were closed but fluttering; her breathing was a steady attempt at keeping things together. When he breathed in, the air pierced against his lung and his whole body shivered. He thought about that soap star and that first shower. He thought about all the Sundays after that and how they were replaced with a kid and a life that he wanted nothing more than to just keep living. He thought about how he had the key to living that life in his arms right now and she had just told him to stop. Just...to stop.

But he couldn't do that. *Don'tcha get it, Hollie? I can't just stop. I've been trying to stop for months now. Years even. Probably longer than we've ever been together, but I can't even know that. I made you my* world *when we got together—there was enough light from you to make that a worthwhile way to live. But eventually I just couldn't anymore. Eventually, I slipped up and—and—and—*

Tyler let out another wail from down the hall.

"Go," sputtered Hollie, "Go help him."

"Everything is fine," Nathan said. He wasn't even sure he was responding to her anymore.

"He needs you."

"*You* need me."

"No." She met his eyes. It looked like she wanted to say more. Then she shook her head and lowered her gaze again. "No, just...no. Please, Nathan."

He stood there for a minute that felt like an hour, trapped in the silence that surrounded them. Hollie didn't look up. He hardly breathed. Until finally, he had no choice but to take a small step backwards and reach his hand out behind him. He found the door and sidestepped it. "I'll be back," he said.

Hollie was standing now. She used the bed frame to pull her weight the rest of the way up. Her legs looked like they were made of jelly. She turned to him and nodded. "I know. I'll be asleep. So, goodnight."

He turned and ran without another word.

Tyler wailed on through the night.

Nathan placed his now empty whiskey glass in the sink and ran the water over the rim until the glass was overflowing. He would rinse it tomorrow. He liked to let his glasses soak after he'd been drinking. He found it gave them a more thorough clean. That way, if Tyler wanted apple juice or something, he could use the same glass without worry. He kept the alcohol on a shelf no step stool could help the little man reach. The last thing he wanted was for him to taste what daddy was sipping on every night.

Every night. He shook his head. Landry told him his drinking had become a *crutch* a long time ago. Well, if that were the case and he was down to three-sips-to-smooth, then what had his crutch turned into now? He'd just give it a rest for the next few nights. That way he could tell Landry he was taking a break, she could tell him she was extra proud of him, and he could smile ruefully from across the cramped little office she had him join her in every week. *That* was all he needed.

He walked away from the sink and moved to the couch just as the split arrived. It ran down from the top of his hairline to right between his eyes. It happened whenever he drank whiskey on an empty stomach—he could've sworn he had eaten something, but what it was escaped him now—and usually carried on to the next day. It wasn't the piercing kind of split—he and Tyler had gotten to calling every headache a split because Tyler didn't like the word ache, and he said it sometimes felt like his skull was splitting in two—but a reminder on a low simmer that his body needed something he wasn't providing enough of. Water, food, sober nights, who really knew? He just knew the split was where all the bad stuff lived. The memories of those last few months with Hollie after they had finally decided to call it quits. The day he moved into the city, rather than the suburb they'd built a life in together. It was just a forty minute, maybe slightly longer, drive, but Hollie had told him it wouldn't be possible for him to see Tyler that often anymore. Just the weekends, usually.

"That hardly seems fair, Babe—Hollie."

She had no nickname now. She was just Hollie. Simple, really.

"It is fair," was her only retort. And he supposed in a way it was. Even if it wasn't—who was he to argue, really?

And so that became reality. Tyler came and visited over the weekends (some of them, mostly over the summer, and far fewer during the school year) and stayed with his mom during the week. He grew up and Nathan grew older. He found his first grey hair just a month after the divorce was final; he had a whole head of pre-mature greying by the end of that year. Online, guys told him they liked the greying look. It seemed to turn them on. To Nathan, it was a cursed reminder that he'd given up something great and lost even more in the process.

He settled onto his side and tucked a pillow under his head. His feet crossed over the arm of the couch but didn't droop down. The middle of his couch sloped inward, so much so that at some point it would need replacing. During one of his recent visits, Tyler had been jumping on the center—something he was instructed *never* to do—and broke the structure. The boy had cried, and Nathan had comforted him, all the while seeing dollar signs fading from behind his eyes.

There goes another bonus check—

He pulled his blanket over to his shoulders and

reached an arm forward to grab the remote off the ottoman.

FWOOMP! Upstairs, a door slammed shut. Nathan turned his head, ready to chalk it up to the wind and nothing more when—

"AHHHHH!"

Nathan's back went rigid. "Tyler?!"

He stood up and his blanket fell around his ankles. It grabbed at his ankle as he lumbered forward and stopped him mid-stride. He stumbled forward and caught himself just before slamming against the carpet. His back was bent, and he felt a loud *creeeaaak* in his spine as he straightened up again. Christ, he was gonna feel that in the morning. Not now though—for now, the whiskey numbed any pain from truly igniting."Tyler!?"

Tyler had been sound asleep just an hour ago. His breathing had been even and slow by the time Nathan had one foot out the door after tucking him in. And he was a sound sleeper, too. The kind who, once he was asleep, liked to stay that way. He was a good kid through and through. A good kid who liked a good sleep and making sure his daddy got a good one without interruption too—

"AHHHHH!"

"Tyler! Tyler!" Nathan raced up the stairs, tripped up the third from the top, spat out a curse at the blasted thing and crawled on his hands and knees up the last two before cracking his back again and slamming a hand against the right wall to drag himself onto his feet. The whiskey pulsed at the back of his head. "Tyler!"

The kid let out another scream just as Nathan reached his door. He shot a hand in first and flicked on the lights.

Tyler sat bolt straight on his bed, blankets up to his chin and a wide-eyed, horrified look stretched across his face. He turned to Nathan and looked ready to scream again. His mouth gaped, his eyes bulged, but instead of screaming, he shut them tight and started to cry. He pulled the blanket up over his face and let out a wail. "Daddy! Daddy get him out!"

Nathan kneeled at his son's bed. "Tyler, *shh, shh,* it's okay."

He hated that the first thing he thought was what the neighbors might be hearing. The window was open, and a soft breeze curled the tips of Nathan's bangs. Had anybody on the block heard the screaming? Had they thought to call the cops? The last thing he needed was Hollie to catch wind of an after-hours cop car rolling up the driveway while Tyler was here. That would be the last time Tyler got to spend the weekend with his daddy, that was for damn sure.

He brushed a hand against his son's leg. "Tyler, Tyler what happened?"

The boy's whole body was shaking. He sniffled once, twice, and then fought to breathe in. He shook his head as he lifted it out from behind the blanket. Nathan guided the sheet down around Tyler's lap. Tyler lifted a shaking arm and pointed at his closet. "He—he—" Then he broke down again, keeled over into his blanket and sobbed.

"Shh, it's alright." Nathan stroked his boy's head. He had Hollie's soft blonde curls that made him look like a cherub. "There's nothing in there that can hurt you."

The closet was a fear Nathan was prepared for. He'd read about it in all the child-rearing books he'd picked up post-divorce. It felt more pertinent then to make a strong impression on his son. The chapters on fears rang through his head now. Closets, under the bed, attics, basements, anywhere dark and scary that had leaping shadows and unidentifiable objects. They were common fears that just took time to break free of. Time and support. *Lots* of support.

"It's just a closet. Do you want Daddy to show you that it isn't scary?"

"*NO!*"

"Tyler, it's okay. I promise you." Nathan turned toward the closet.

As he did, a shadow raced across the sliver of space between the door and carpet.

Nathan's heart skipped a beat.

He turned back to his son, then back to the closet. When he squinted, he couldn't make out any movement. But he knew what he'd seen. Something had shifted from behind the door. Something was in there.

Daddy, get him out!

Or someone...

His eyes flicked to the open window. There was no screen on it ever since a particularly bad storm that spring had knocked the thing out. Nathan had planned to get it replaced for months; it just never happened. For a flashing second, he pictured someone climbing through the window into his son's room. No —no that wasn't possible. It was a second-story window without a tree or a balcony to scale. There was nothing to cling to that would provide enough grip. And yet—

He looked back at the closet, eyes honed on the gap beneath the door.

"Daddy..."

Tyler's voice broke his steely gaze. He turned to him and smiled weakly. "It's all okay, kiddo. I—" he looked back and checked for moving shadows, "I can show you."

"No, no daddy please. No he's in there. He's—"

"Nobody's in there, Ty. I promise."

He stood and started walking toward the door. Tyler's cries for him to stop faded as Nathan reached out a hand for the doorknob. He kept staring at the gap between the door and the carpet. As he was just a few inches from the door, he saw another flash of movement. And then, he heard a creak from the other side of the door.

Tyler yelped from his bed. Nathan's breath caught in his throat. A creak? No, not possible. There was no one in this house but them. He made sure of it. Every night he locked the doors—back door first, front door second—and always made sure it was just them. It had always been just them ever since he and Hollie separated. It was just them tonight, too. There was no *him* to get out of the closet. There was only Nathan and his son. Nathan and his son and nobody else. Nobody hiding behind the—

He twisted the handle.

Tyler squirmed in bed behind him.

Nathan threw open the door.

He let out a breath.

The closet was empty on the other side. Nathan reached in, flicked on the light, and then bent over to pick up a sweater that had fallen off one of the shelves. He held it out as he turned back to Tyler. "See? Nothing to be worried about."

Tyler was unconvinced. He wore his skepticism like a shield as Nathan walked back to him and sat on the edge of his bed. "You know," he said, "you were pretty brave not to run." This was something else he read in those books. You have to make the kid feel normal for being scared. You sometimes have to make them feel grown up. "A lot of kids your age would've run out that door and down the stairs to get me. Heck, I probably would've done the same."

"I saw him..."

"Saw who?"

"Th-the..." he sniffled, "the Lop-Sided man."

"The what?"

But Tyler didn't respond. He reached over to his nightstand and pulled open the drawer. Crinkled construction paper and loose pens and pencils littered the drawer. Tyler had picked up drawing right around Christmas of last year. Nathan had gotten him a sketchpad per request of Hollie (*"You'll be the best dad ever if you get him this, it's all he's talked about the last few weeks."*), and the kid had taken off since then. He pulled out the top page and laid it on the bed. He pushed it toward Nathan.

"What is this?" He picked up the page and felt his mouth go dry.

"That's the Lop-Sided man."

The Lop-Sided man was a series of jagged lines and harsh edges that made up the image of a face. A face with a long torso, equally long legs, and one long arm. The other arm was half the size and dangled uselessly at the man's side. The long arm reached up and out, almost like it was trying to grab something, or someone, just outside of the picture. His face had two eyes, but no mouth or nose. He wore a cap on his head, something like a fedora. And his head was tilted down.

Nathan looked at his boy. "You drew this?"

Tyler nodded.

"*Why* did you draw this?"

"I don't know. I wasn't trying to. He just appeared."

Appeared...

Nathan handed the paper back to Tyler, but the boy didn't grab it. It sat between them on the bed until a small breeze pushed it an inch closer to Tyler. The boy snagged it and shoved it back into the drawer. "I didn't want to draw him. I just did."

Nathan couldn't tell if Tyler was ashamed or nervous or what expression was painted across his face. He looked almost pained with the way his temples crinkled and his forehead pulled taut. It added years onto the five-year-old's face. Nathan reached out and draped an arm across Tyler's shoulder. He pulled him in closer. The wrinkles faded, and Tyler met his gaze. "And that's who you saw in the closet?"

Tyler nodded.

A chill ran down Nathan's spine and he had the distinct feeling something was watching him. He peered over his shoulder at the lit closet behind him. There was no Lop-Sided man standing in the doorway with his one long arm and lifeless, yellow eyes. There were just clothes and a few toys and a stuffed animal or two that Nathan had bought for Tyler just for him to not really like them much. He thought about grabbing one for him to snuggle with tonight. *Hell, maybe I could use one for tonight.* But he didn't move to get up. Instead he turned back to his son and said, "Well, he's not there anymore. Right?"

Tyler pulled away from his dad and glanced again at the closet. Then, he nodded. "Right."

Nathan got up and went to close the closet. "And he's not gonna be there the rest of tonight, either. And if he is...he's got you and me to answer to!" Nathan held up both his fists at the closet and made at punching the air around the door before closing it. Tyler laughed.

With the closet door shut, Nathan made his way back to Tyler's bed. "Are you gonna be alright here tonight?"

The boy flicked his eyes to the closet, but his smile didn't falter. "Yes!"

Nathan nodded. "Good. I'm gonna close the window too. It's too windy tonight anyways." The wind was clearly what had slammed the door shut in the first place. Tyler's imagination had taken it from there. Nathan knew how these things went. Without the wind, and with the door shut like it should've been before, Tyler was going to struggle to fall asleep, but still get there in the end. It was late, and the boy looked tired. His imagination wouldn't be strong enough to keep him up much longer if his drooping eyelids were any indicator.

"Okay." Tyler tucked himself back into bed and pulled the covers up to his chin. When the window was closed, Nathan turned around and planted a kiss on his son's forehead.

"Sleep tight, kiddo. Tomorrow Mommy comes to pick you up."

Normally, Tyler would moan that he wanted to stay with daddy or didn't sleep well with Mommy or any number of things when their time together was drawing closed. This time, though, Nathan saw something else flash behind Tyler's eyes, and he felt a pang in his chest. Tyler didn't fight the statement and instead just closed his eyes and said, "I'm tired, daddy."

"I know," he said back. "I know. Sweet dreams, kid. I'll see you in the morning."

He circled the bed and went to turn out the lights. Once he flicked them off, the dim light from the moon was all that glowed in the darkened room. Tyler rolled over in bed and then rolled back again. He was still troubled, no doubt, but he didn't speak up. He was gonna be okay. He was a strong kid after all. Besides, there was nothing to be scared of in that room. Nothing to be scared of at all.

Nathan turned down the darkened hallway and descended the stairs. It wasn't until he got back to the couch and wrapped himself in his own blanket that he remembered shutting the closet door the first time he'd tucked Tyler in that night.

He remembered the slam.

Just the wind, he had thought.

And that was probably true. But the closet shouldn't have been open in the first place. How in the hell had it been propped open?

Nathan didn't sleep a wink that night.

He was too busy listening for footsteps.

2

Rebecca Landry clicked her pen twice and set it gently inside her evergreen moleskin notebook. Across the room, the oscillating fan ruffled the notebook's pages. Nathan watched them flip, one over top of another, until the pen was only visible from its black, pointed tip. It had been left clicked open, and the bulbous ink on the tip bubbled up like a dark, looming shadow.

Tick...tock...tick...tock...

The analog overhead boomed loudly through the silence. The pen was barely visible. So was the shadow that flitted along the bottom of the closet doorframe. He thought he heard a scream, even as he knew it wasn't there. *It's in the past, Nathan. In the past.* But then he thought he heard another. Ear-splitting, high pitched. The scream of a child sitting up in bed, staring through a dark room at a door that wasn't left ajar. Nathan glanced toward the office door and rubbed the back of his neck. The place smelled of bamboo and eucalyptus. It must've been giving him a rash. Probably something simple he could pick up a cream for on his way home today. That way, it would be cleared up by next Friday when Tyler was back in town. He could tuck Tyler in, and the boy wouldn't notice his hands were beet red and the back of his neck was splotchy. Not that he would notice, either way.

He would be too busy staring at the closet door.

At the Lop-Sided man.

"Nathan—Nathan—"

He blinked twice and shook his head. The Lop-Sided man vanished to the back of his subconscious. He still felt him there, running a thin, splintery finger along the ripples of his mind.

"Nathan."

He focused on the chair across from him. Landry sat with her chin resting on her open palm, propped up by her elbow against the chair-side table. A single strand of dark, copper hair fell across her forehead.

"Sorry," he said. "I, er—didn't sleep much last night."

She nodded. "That's understandable." She bent forward and flipped the pages back in her notebook. She read something she'd just jotted down. "And you were on the couch?"

He swallowed the lump of saliva at the top of his throat. "I do that sometimes."

"By choice?"

He nodded.

She waited.

Christ, he hated the waiting.

"I just...I find it easier," he said. Which she, of course, knew was bullshit. But it wasn't, not entirely. It was easier to fall asleep on the couch some nights than to drag himself up the stairs to the bedroom, where he slept alone in a bed big enough for two. Landry looked back a few pages, probably to her notes from a different session. He could've sworn he had told her that at some point. Why his sleep always came up, he wasn't sure. They shouldn't be talking about his sleep now. Not when Tyler was the one who couldn't sleep through the night anymore.

"Right...and Tyler," she said. "Did he fall back asleep? You know, after?" The notebook was in her lap now. The pen was tucked between two fingers like a 1920s cigarillo. She tapped it against her chin and waited.

"I-I'm not sure. I think so."

He shuffled in his chair.

"That's good."

"He's a good kid."

"I'm sure. He sounds wonderful, Nathan."

Nathan. He hated when she used his name like that. Like they were some kind of friend any deeper than a paid acquaintance. He noticed for the first time how far she had made it into the journal. Hadn't she just started a new one when they first met all those months ago?

Tick...tock...

He looked again at the clock. Landry shifted in her seat and drew his attention back. "How has work been lately?"

"Fine," he said. "Work's always fine."

Nathan had started his job with General Motors as a Claims Processing Manager just a few months after moving out of the old house. At first, before the job transfer, he'd been determined to stay in the area. For the first year or so he rented a small studio on a month-to-month lease. The fees were astronomical and the space was tiny, but he was just a few blocks away from Tyler and Hollie and the apartment was convenient for making himself available whenever they needed. His old job was still in the area, and his commute was the kind of bearable torture that every early morning drive to a sterile, poorly lit office ought to be. And best yet, Tyler loved the place. He had been four years old and his curiosity was piqued by the entire space. *Where's the other rooms, Daddy? You don't have a couch, Daddy; do you want ours? I'm almost as tall as this now. See?* He stood next to the kitchen counter and held a hand above his head. It hovered a few inches above the top of his hairline, perfectly parallel with the countertop. *You are,* Nathan told him. Then he would scoop him up in his arms and toss him onto the mattress just a few feet away. Tyler would giggle and tumble through the blankets until he was wrapped in a big, Tyler-sized burrito. Nathan would then leap onto the other side of the bed and send the boy rocketing up. Sometimes he would scream. Sometimes he would laugh. Always he would smile and then call out *again again! Daddy do it again!* And most of the time, Nathan was happy to oblige. Then, after the rest of the night had passed and a final call to Hollie had been made, they would fall asleep in the bed together. Usually, Tyler would hog all the blankets, but Nathan never minded.

When he got the job with GM and could finally work from home, it was time to put the studio life behind him. He found a house for rent on the other side of town within budget and jumped on it. Now, he lived an hour from his old office and an hour and a half from his old life.

"And how was the date last week?"

He laughed. "It didn't happen."

"What? But that was all you talked about last week. Didn't you have that feeling things might actually work out." Landry flipped a few pages back. "I swear I wrote that exact thing down."

"I had to cancel. Emergency Tyler visit. Hollie

couldn't get a sitter. The guy said he understood, then didn't reply the next day. I haven't talked to him since. I don't know if he *really* knew what dating a guy with a kid would be like."

Probably because you kept it off your profile.

"Hmm, well, that's a shame. It can be fun to date. You're single. You live alone. This is your chance to really write your own next chapter."

Nathan shrugged.

Landry's eyes narrowed. "You're not saying much today, Nathan."

"Sorry. I guess I'm just still just thinking about Tyler."

"About last night?"

"Yeah...and other nights. He's been sleeping worse and worse every time he visits me."

"And you think they're related?"

"Not necessarily." Which really meant: *Yes.*

"When does he come visit next?" Landry was writing furiously, and Nathan wondered if it was possible for a pen to spontaneously combust from too much pressure.

"Two weeks. He's with his mom until then."

"*Hmph.* Plenty of time to get over the night terrors, then."

Night terrors. The label made the whole thing seem trivial. The folded-up papers in his back pocket weren't trivial though. He bent forward and reached around to grab them. Landry's gaze followed his hand as he extended it forward and passed off his son's drawings.

"He showed me these the other night, too."

Landry flipped through each one like it was a memory in an old scrapbook. She paused on the one of the Lop-Sided man, looked up at Nathan, then back down again. She went to flip to the next when the fan sputtered out. A strong gust of wind picked up the top drawing and flew it toward the closed door. Nathan got up and reached for it.

"So sorry," Landry was saying. Nathan hardly heard her, though. He grabbed the scribbled-out picture of the Lop-Sided man and shoved it back in his pocket. The back of his pants burned as he sat back down.

"All good," he said.

Landry straightened the rest of the drawings and passed them back. "They're certainly creative," she said. "When did he start drawing?"

"Last year."

"He's very talented."

"They, uh, weren't always like this." He looked down at the top sketch. At the center of the page was a roughly drawn rectangle. The lines were jagged and harsh, the same kinds of lines that made up the Lop-Sided man in his drawing. At the bottom of the rectangle was a series of thinner, sharper lines jutting out like sun rays. A circle was at the center, off to the right of the drawing. "This one's a door."

"I see that," said Landry. She didn't say anything else. Probably because she was thinking the same thing Nathan had thought since he found the drawings earlier that day. He had gone digging through the top drawer of Tyler's nightstand and could've sworn he steadied his breath at least three, maybe four times. The first was when he saw just how many drawings of the Lop-Sided man there were. He brought only the one Tyler had shown him last night, but there were at least ten buried beneath the other sketches of closet doors, open windows, lonely beds in empty bedrooms. One of them—one of the ones Nathan *did* bring with him today—showed a small boy sitting up in a bed. The boy had no face, but he had one short arm to the left and another, much longer arm on the right. Behind him was a circular moon outside a slanted window.

The subtext was potent.

"Plenty of kids are afraid of plenty of things," said Landry. "They always grow out of them."

"Right." What didn't feel right was how Nathan couldn't stop thinking about those same fears now, or how certain he had been just last night that Tyler wasn't just afraid of the dark.

There had been someone on the other side of that door.

Someone or something.

An alarm sounded from Landry's phone. "Oh!" She shut the sound off before it could loop for the second time. "That's our hour."

Nathan took a deep breath. "Thank you again for your time."

"No, no, my pleasure. It's always great to hear how things are going with you."

Even when you don't believe a single word of it.

Nathan stood and shoved the rest of the pictures into his pocket. He'd return them to Tyler's drawer before the boy came back. He knew how particular kids were at this age, and also how observant. He would notice a few papers out of place.

Or a shadow under a door.

Landry reached a hand out, and Nathan gave it a shake. He stepped out of her way then as she reached the same hand out to the door knob. Outside, the lobby was bright and drenched in the heavy silence of a hospital waiting room. There was a woman waiting on a grey chair with a book in hand and an oversized handbag on the seat next to her. She looked up when Landry walked out. She raised a hand and mouthed, *Hi.* Nathan gave her an awkward smile and skirted her gaze.

"Same time next week," Landry said.

"Same time next week."

He was almost out the door when Landry called out and said, "Oh and, Nathan." He turned back around. "Keep those drawings. Trust me, as a parent, one day you'll be thankful for them."

Nathan called his old landline as he drove home that day.

Sometimes he missed having a home phone. It made a place feel official, he thought, to have a phone number associated with it. Growing up, he still remembered the rush he would get when his parents' old landline would start to ring. It was plugged into the wall back then—still was probably, though he hadn't visited longer than an hour or so since the divorce; it was hard to muster up the strength their bombardment of questions was going to take just to manage—and little Nathan would sputter barefoot across tiled floors to see what number was calling. He had Grandma's number memorized before he even knew their own. He also knew the first three digits of his school's number, and that meant it was time to run.

Hollie still had the same phone number they had together. *248-680*...it felt familiar just to dial it.

She picked up the call on the second ring.

"Hello?"

The gruff voice on the other line did not belong to

Hollie. Nathan's heart sunk. "Hi, Mrs. Smart. It's Nathan."

Lorelei Smart was the kind of woman who never told you how she really felt about you; you just always knew. She wore her hair big and her blush bigger, and she stored secrets like a foraged winter stock in among the bushy curls of her dense and dark hair. Secrets about Nathan, most likely. He hadn't hit it off with his mother-in-law out the gate. Hollie was her only daughter and being originally from a rural pocket of Illinois—now the in-laws lived in Waterford, ten minutes from Hollie and just over an hour from Nathan—family lines ran thick. Nathan spent long years giving perfectly thought-out Christmas presents (which Hollie mainly picked herself), telling his best stories around the dinner table, and surprising with clean-cut and spontaneous appearances on Mrs. Smart's front porch with baked goods in hand and gel swooping his hair to the side. She seemed to really like him by the end, if Hollie was to be believed.

All of that came crumbling down the second he and Hollie filed for divorce.

"Hello, Nathan," she said now. He ran a hand across his forehead and turned the AC in his car up. It was suddenly hotter than the devil's domain. "To what do I owe the honor?"

He grimaced. "I—uh—well..." He had had no reason to call Hollie, other than wanting to see how she was doing. Despite everything, she was still his best friend. Talking to her was sometimes the only slice of normalcy he still had in his life. Not that he did it often. Or ever...Today it just felt like the right thing to do. "I...Tyler left something at my place this weekend. I wanted to stop by and drop it off."

"Are you in the area?"

No.

"I can make the drive."

He heard fussing on the other side of the line. Was Tyler starting to cry? His heart kicked against his chest in response.

"No, no, don't do all that, Nathan. We're quite alright," said Mrs. Smart. "Hollie is still at work. And she doesn't like visitors when she's gone."

Her tone shoehorned into one word. *Visitor.* He pulled his lips taut. "Okay, I understand."

"You see Tyler this week again, don't you?"

"Yes. I do."

"Well then," she let out a breath. "I think that solves that then. It must be so hard on the poor boy, though. All the travel."

"It isn't far."

"Well no, of course not. You just have to wonder—what *does* it do to a kid's psyche to see his parents like this?"

It makes them scream at closet doors with nothing behind them.

"Will you let Hollie know I called?"

"Of course. Good day, Nathan, and God bless you."

The line went dead, and Nathan's radio play swept back through the car's AirPlay system. It was on the country music channel, but he didn't bother to change it. He turned it down low and barely listened the rest of the drive home.

3

"Daddy! Daddy!" Tyler ran head-first into Nathan's abdomen. Nathan grunted and looked down at the boy.

"Whoa there, bud, what's going on?" He brushed aside some of Tyler's curly bangs. His lips were tainted blue, and he held a now empty popsicle stick in one hand. Last time he'd checked, Tyler had had three of them. That had been an hour ago, and Nathan had promptly cut him off after the boy stood on a large rock in one of the neighborhood yards and screamed for no reason other than the sugar coursing through his body demanded it.

The sun dipped soft against the horizon and a golden hue settled across the neighborhood street. A streak of four kids were silhouetted by the fading sun, chasing one another past parked cars and other kids who sat with chalk and drawing pictures in the middle of the road. A duo of them had tapered off from the group and were now in the process of sneaking up behind two of the fathers, who sat in their red and blue foldable chairs, little hands outstretched toward the white cooler between them.

Peter Harring and Oscar Rallings sat facing forward and sipped on their beers. Peter Harring set his drink in the chair's cup holder and reached behind him for his sunglasses; they had fallen off moments before as he let out a big belly laugh at something Oscar had said. When he turned, he saw one of the girls with two fingers under the cooler's outer rim, about to pop it open. As she met Harring's eyes, she screamed and broke into a backwards run, stumbling and laughing her way back into the bushes on the side of her house where a few of her friends giggled, too. Moments later, three girls broke from behind the shrubs and ran back into the street. A boy's head popped out a second after, and he chased after them. *Tag*, Nathan thought, *you're it.*

Tyler tugged at the side of his shirt with sticky popsicle fingers.

"Patrick's dad has sparklers," he said. "Can I do one?"

Nathan glanced at the big, burly man handing out sparklers to some of the kids. The runners slowed and turned in his direction. A few of the chalk artists had now stood up. He was gathering a pied piper sort of crowd and, in minutes would be surrounded. His wife and a few of the other women stood a few feet back. From afar, they looked aloof, but Nathan knew they were paying close attention. Where there was fire, there was a legion of mothers watching.

"Just be safe," he said and sent Tyler off.

He torpedoed across the street and almost bucked into one of the other boys before kicking up enough dust to skid his way to a rapid stop. From there, he was handed a sparkler and immediately started waving it around.

"Let him light it first, bud!" Nathan called. Tyler looked back and waved the stick at him. He waved back.

"Well, he's extra smiley today."

Eliza Shepherd strolled up next to him. Her dark hair was pulled back in a low pony, and she wore a blue T-shirt and extremely short jean shorts—the kind where the pockets stuck out at the bottom.

Nathan nodded. "He's been excited about this for weeks."

When Nathan picked his new neighborhood, it had been important for him to find somewhere with an abundance of kids. *Tyler's gonna meet so many other kids, Hollie. It's a really nice place.* Of course, Hollie had been skeptical at first. The first time she came over and saw boys Tyler's age running in the street Nathan had thought that would start to fade. *"I could've hit them, Nathan,"* she said instead. *"I don't think anyone was watching them at all."* Which of course was untrue. Where there were kids, there were half a dozen adults standing by. Sometimes with kids you just had to be covert about it. The next few visits softened her, though. She waved to Mrs. Parker as she unloaded two daughters and two sons—all under the age of ten; Mrs. Parker had been a busy woman for a number of years—from her slate grey mini van across the street. She heard the universal tinkle of an ice cream truck's tune that came by every Sunday morning and drove right past as she was heaving Tyler's overnight bag into the passenger seat. And slowly Nathan watched his ex-wife grow comfortable with the idea of leaving Tyler there for a few nights a month. Tyler wasn't close to any of the other kids here—how close could you really be when they could only see you a few days out of every month? But he was welcome. The neighborhood block parties had food and drink and popsicles for everyone, and the kids were ready to play with him even if they didn't know him well. That was the beauty of kids. It didn't take a lot for them to turn a stranger into a friend.

"I can tell," said Eliza. "Does he go back to school soon?"

"Next week. Starting Kindergarten."

"Oh my God, that must be so surreal."

Frankly, Nathan was better off not thinking about it. Last year, when Tyler had started pre-school, it had been mind-boggling enough. He took a sip of the Corona one of the dads handed to him earlier. He hated beer, but these days he could drink anything so long as it took some of the edge off.

"Less visits," he said. "Which sucks, but it'll be for the best."

"Your idea or Mom's?"

Nathan looked at her. Eliza had the kind of friendly eyes you wanted to tell things to. Tyler wasn't the only one still searching for a connection in this new neck of the woods. From stories his own parents had told him, having a kid was a great way to socialize with other parents your age. With Tyler visiting so little, there hadn't been consistent playdate opportunities. Eliza was the closest he had to a real friend in the neighborhood, and he saw her, what? Twice a month maybe? She lived next door, so sightings were frequent enough. She would be leaving as he was coming home or vice versa. But that sort of thing didn't lead to stellar interactions when both parties were eager to get where they were going and not too keen on making a pit stop to talk to the loser next door, who never stopped to speak to them in the first place.

Last Christmas she brought cookies over to everyone on the street. They'd been pretty good, too. He had waited until Tyler came and visited and let him try them too. In return, Nathan baked peppermint bark and handed it out just to her and the very few neighbors whose faces he would recognize when they answered the door. She invited him in that day, told him Ethan, her husband, was just about wrapped with dinner if he wanted to join them. He didn't want to intrude. End of month was coming at work, and he had some reports to wrap up before Monday morning. It was one of those true excuses that came out smoothly even though he went home afterwards with zero intention of working on that Friday night. He flopped into bed and turned on some documentary that he couldn't even remember now and poured himself a drink.

At one point, Hollie asked if he was making friends. *"It seems like a nice neighborhood,"* she told him. This had been after plenty of visits had proven that to her. *"Go out and make some friends. Maybe invite a few of them over for the holidays."*

That had been how Nathan found out he wasn't coming home for the holidays. He had figured as much. Hollie would bring Tyler to her parents' house, and then he'd get to celebrate with the little bugger later in the week. During his pre-scheduled weekend visit.

"I've got holiday plans already," he told her that day.

"Oh? Well, good. I'm glad." It had been a lie, but one of those necessary ones everyone told to turn someone's pity to confusion. He didn't want Hollie's pity. He didn't need it. That holiday, he sat home alone and watched Miracle on 34th Street. His parents thought he was at Hollie's. Hollie thought he was with them. The

world forgot about him for a moment, and he found he didn't mind.

"Her idea," he finally said. "But I think it'll be good for him to be in one place for longer so he can focus on school and making friends out there. There's a little league soccer group I think Hollie wants to sign him up for. Get some of that energy out."

Tyler's sparkler was lit now. He jumped back when the thing first started sparking, and Nathan smiled. Then, he watched his son wave it in a delicate figure-8 out in front of him, as the burly father was instructing all the kids to do. They stood a few feet apart, nobody's clothes sparked up and caught fire, and even though the horde of mothers were now moving closer, no accidents occurred. Nathan's breath was still tight, though. What would Hollie think if Tyler came home with a burn mark?

That was something nobody told you about divorced parents: how easy it was to turn a best friend into an adversary.

"Well lemme know if he needs any pointers?"

"You played little league?"

"And other things," she laughed. "I was on the soccer team all through college. Forward, mostly, so I was scoring the goals."

"Okay, look at you go."

She made a show of mock curtseying to accept the compliment. Eliza was *not* one of the parents in the neighborhood, even though Nathan was pretty certain she and him shared a graduation year. When she turned her head, her ponytail flicked with a sort of youthful wave that he wondered if he still had in him. *You're twenty-nine...*he told himself. He wasn't decrepit yet.

"Seriously though, if he does play and you need a buddy for the games, I'm so down."

"I could see you being a soccer mom."

"Is that a dig?"

He shook his head. "No, just...do you want kids?"

"Eventually." She took a sip from her Fanta orange soda. "Ethan's not ready right now. He says it wouldn't work out to do that now. Fine by me. There's plenty of stuff I want to do before a kid enters the picture."

"I feel that..."

Nathan then watched as Tyler dunked his rapidly shortening sparkler in a bucket of water near his feet and raced across the street towards them. "Daddy! Daddy! Did you see?"

"I did, bud. Looked great. Doh!" He ran into Nathan again, full force. His body was practically vibrating with excitement.

"It was sooo cool. It was fire in my hands."

"Like a magic wand," said Eliza.

Tyler turned to her. "What's that?"

She bent down so she was eye level with the kid. "It's something only witches and wizards get to use. It's a wooden stick about yay big." She held up her fingers to indicate how long the stick was. "And they can cast magical spells out of it. Witches like to turn princes into frogs. Wizards like to disappear so you can't see them." Tyler stood mesmerized as Eliza spoke, and when she was done, he turned to Nathan and tugged at his shirt corner again.

"Daddy I want a magic wand."

"Okay okay, we'll getcha one for your birthday, how 'bout that?"

"Oh is your birthday coming up soon?" asked Eliza.

"November," said Nathan.

"That's closer than you think."

"Really?" said Tyler.

"Mmhm, it'll be here before you know it."

After that, Tyler ran off to light another sparkler and play tag with some of the slightly bigger kids. "Be careful!" Nathan shouted. Then, to Eliza, he said, "You'll *definitely* be good with kids."

"Ya think?"

"Based off the last two minutes, yeah I do."

"Well, I'll get to convincing Ethan of that any day now. Probably after one of his D&D games. He usually drinks a lot during those. I bet he'll be much easier to sway."

"He plays D&D?"

"Every week. Sunday evenings. You should come by."

The idea was almost laughable. "Oh no, I don't play."

"Oh please! You couldn't pay me to play. I tried once when Ethan and I were still in college. It went horribly. All his friends were talking in these weird voices, and one of them even came wearing this heavy cloak thing with fur over the shoulders. Where do you even get something like that?"

"I'm pretty sure there's shops for it."

"Yeah, not my scene. And I was *very* ill-prepared. They had fun though. It's the same group he gets together with now."

"Oh that's fun."

"Yeah," she shrugged. "But anyways, a bunch of the wives of the guys he plays with come over and we all hang out. Penny comes from a few doors down too, and her husband wouldn't be caught dead pretending to be an orc or elf or whatever. Probably an orc for him. He's got that stature, you know?"

Now, Nathan did laugh. "What do you all do?"

"Just hang out. They play in the basement so we've got the rest of the house to ourselves. Usually drink some wine. I'll get a movie going or something, but usually we just talk. It's hard to make friends as an adult. This just makes it a little bit easier."

It seems like a nice neighborhood...go out and make some friends...

"This Sunday?"

"Usually around 6? Is Tyler outta your hair by then?"

"Not this week, and I've got, uh a thing the week after. I think." Eliza's face turned to skepticism. "I'll let you know if that changes though."

"Totally do. We'd love to have you. Truly."

He nodded, but already his mind was a Rolodex of reasons he couldn't make it. Why was he like this these days? Hadn't he loved going out back in college? He used to know all of Hollie's friends; she knew all of his. The only times they were alone were when they intentionally set out to not see anybody else, and even then, that never lasted long. Now, he looked at Eliza as she drank the last of her soda and then tapped her red-polished nails along the aluminum can, and his head filled with skepticism.

*We'd love to have you. Truly...*He shook his head and turned back to his son who now twirled two sparklers, one in each hand, with the same burly father standing guard behind him. The dad looked up and waved at Nathan. He wasn't sure he knew him, but he smiled and waved back anyways. Tyler did not look up. His face was a mask of concentration as the sparks flew out on either side of him and the setting sun stretched his shadow long out in front of him on the road. The shadow reminded him of something, a drawing, where a man could stretch one arm long and reach out from around the closet door, but he didn't let that thought nest tonight. Tonight, all was well. There was no scary monster in the closet, just a setting sun and a couple of sparklers dancing in the growing dusk.

SEPTEMBER

4

———

It can be fun to date...write your next chapter...you're single...you live alone...

Yeah, thought Nathan. *And I should've stayed at home tonight.*

Two weeks had passed since Tyler's last visit, and Nathan was finally putting himself out there the way Dr. Landry kept encouraging him to do. During their last session, she hadn't shut up about it. *Don't you ever think about what else could be out there?* Yes—he had to admit he did, but that wasn't enough of a reason to break the routine he had built for himself. Besides, lately, he had finally started to feel comfortable enough in said routine to crack open another note-book and start jotting down some ideas for a new story. He had a good feeling about this one, too. He was inching closer to thirty, and by thirty he swore he would have something out there. It didn't matter who read it. It didn't matter who liked it. What mattered is they *could* read it and *could* like it if they felt so in-clined. He just needed to open those doors.

And he wasn't opening any doors by sitting alone in a bar on a random Thursday night thinking, not about the man he had agreed to meet here, but about his therapist. After their last talk, he had gone home and poured himself an extra strong whiskey on ice. He took it to bed with him—not the couch, mind you—and set it on his nightstand. There, he flopped onto bed and pulled out his phone. Try dating again, he thought. Had he *dated* Hollie ever before they were together? He could remember *dates,* but they had already been together for those. When had they made it official?

The way he saw it, nobody dated these days anyways. They just talked because it was something to pass the time until something better came along. He sighed and sipped at his whiskey. The glass was cool with condensation. *Just something to pass the time*, he thought as his finger hovered over his most recently downloaded app. It was his most recent because he deleted it once every three or four days before downloading it again. He pressed down to open it again and the familiar mix of alluring dread resurfaced.

Grindr was a strange place. It had taken him all of six months of being out and on his own before trying the app for the first time. It took him just one night to decide it probably wasn't the place for him. It was a place where faceless profiles could message you and tell you everything they would do to your body if given the chance. A place where you saw your neighbor's husbands or colleagues from work and pretended you were unaware the next time you saw them in real life. *What brings you on here?* you could ask. *What do you do for work?* Eventually they might respond, or sometimes they wouldn't. Didn't mean the conversation was done though. They might skirt the innocuous questions all together and lead with a picture, or two, or three, of whatever parts of their body they wanted to show.

And sometimes, through it all you could find someone normal enough to put together a bio that mentioned they liked classical music, moved from *Nevada* of all places, and was now a hardcore Detroit Lions fan. And if you were lucky, you could then invite that normal person out for a drink on a random Thursday night in September.

As long as they remembered to show.

Nathan checked his watch again. 9:10. Ten minutes was nothing, though. Ten minutes could still mean he was on his way. The traffic had been terrible downtown, and he had said he was coming from out that way. Nathan had offered to pick him up, but he had denied the gesture. Honestly, that was more green flag if anything. It meant he had his own car, and it meant he didn't intrinsically trust strangers on the internet. Nathan liked that.

He twirled the glass of ice water with the little black straw usually reserved for alcoholic drinks. He had his elbows propped up on the counter and twisted over his shoulder to stare at the door. A younger woman walked in with a few friends close behind. They were laughing and putting away their IDs. One of them looked almost too young to have made it inside. *College students*, Nathan thought, and he tried to remember what that phase of life had been like. He and Hollie were never the party types. While everyone else went out, they would stay in and watch a movie, or play a board game, or just spend their night in splitting a bottle of wine and laughing.

Nathan hadn't had wine since leaving Hollie.

He preferred to leave that in the past too.

Behind the girls, a man walked in with his head down. He wore a distressed jean jacket and black pants. They were tight. When he looked up, Nathan saw past his mop of shaggy brown hair and smiled. He lifted a hand and went to stand up. His feet tangled in the bar stool's footrest for a second, and he felt awkward as he detached from the stool and leaned back against the bar. By then, the man was in front of him. He was smiling.

You have a great smile by the way, Nathan had told him after a few meager messages had become a full blown conversation. They had talked about Nevada, where this man was from, and how he made it to the Midwest of all places from the state of sin.

Just the city of sin. The rest of the state is perfectly normal. If you like deserts. Which I didn't. So I ended up here.

Home of the great plains and the great lakes.

And I've been impressed with both so far.

Now, Nathan's mouth was suddenly dry. Travis's smile was just as cute as it had been online. No, cuter somehow. One side of his mouth quirked up higher than the other, and he had a slight bucktoothed look without any rodent comparisons coming to mind. He was young and he looked it, but Nathan reminded himself he wasn't that much older—six years was nothing once you passed a certain age—and tried to choke out an awkward hello.

Travis beat him to it.

"Hi," he said. He went in for a hug and Nathan happily obliged. Travis's body was warm but not sweaty. Nathan's hands felt suddenly clammy.

"Hey, fancy meeting you here."

Travis laughed.

"Thanks for that," said Nathan.

"Of course." He sidestepped him and moved to the barstool next to him. "Always happy to hand out some pity laughs."

"Oh, so that's how it's gonna be?"

Travis slid onto the seat just as the bartender came up. "Are you drinking?"

"Uh no no, I've got an early meeting tomorrow."

"Okay, no worries." Then, to the bartender he said, "I'll take a gin and tonic. He's driving." There was such a casual way he tilted his head at the bartender while leaning slightly over the counter that it made Nathan think Travis already knew him. Which of course wasn't possible. Travis had suggested this place because he had never been before, and he wanted to try something new. *I think it's fun to see new things with new people...* Nathan sat down next to him and took a sip of his ice water.

"So," he said, "how was your day?"

They spent the next two hours at the bar. Travis held conversation with a skill well beyond his twenty-three years. In that two hours, Nathan learned about his degree—music composition and political science; *the poli sci was so I could actually get a job when all was said and done*—his friends, his family—*Irina's two years older, Cece's four younger...Mom and Dad swear she wasn't an accident buuutt*—and why he came to the Midwest for work and how he just decided one day in his first month here that he would probably never leave it.

"Sometimes you can just, I don't know, *tell*. There's no proof; you just know."

Through it all, Nathan smiled and laughed and eventually ordered himself a whiskey and coke (though instinct told him to drop the coke, just add extra ice) while the two talked. He told Travis about his own college experience, then about work and how he could constantly manage being home all day, every day. "You have to get out," he told the younger man. "But I like walks anyways. They keep me fit."

"They do." Travis nodded in agreement.

It made Nathan blush. He took another sip of whiskey and tried not to scan too low down on Travis's tight body. His shirt puckered near his pecs and tapered in with his thin waist. When he laughed, his waist crunched in, and Nathan almost swore he saw a set of abs under the tight material. He crossed his legs under the bar.

"So, you have a son?"

Nathan had just finished his drink and was chasing it with his now lukewarm water. Travis was nursing his second gin but slowing down. "I do," said Nathan. "Tyler." He braced himself for the conversation, which had been so light and fresh all night, to suddenly turn sour.

"How old is he?" Travis's finger traced the outer rim of his glass.

"Five."

"Damn," said Travis. "You got to it fast."

Nathan nearly choked on his water. "I wouldn't say it like that..."

"I'm kidding," said Travis. His eyes twinkled in the bar's dim light. Nathan had never seen blue eyes quite so shocking before. "I bet he's great."

"He is."

"Does he live with you?"

"His mom. He visits every two weeks though. Sort of. He's in school now, so maybe a little less. It depends."

"I get that. I bet you miss him when he's not around, though."

"Usually. I still talk to him on the phone at least once a week. More if I'm lucky. I don't know. Things are busy. But that usually means I'm glad it's just me at home."

A silence settled over the two of them. Travis took another sip and then slid the glass further away. His dark blue eyes never left Nathan's own. He fought to keep his gaze steady.

"It's a nice home."

"I bet. Mid-Century modern, you said?"

"To a point."

"Well, I'd love to see it."

And Nathan realized he would love for him to see it too. "You're welcome any time," he said. Then he cleared his throat and added, "Even now."

Travis arched his brows, but the smile never left his lips. His two lips were uneven in a charming way. The bottom was much fuller than the top. For a second, Travis's tongue flicked across his top lip; Nathan followed its path. "I'd love that." He watched Travis's mouth form the words and felt his own smile creep up. He stood suddenly from the chair and called the bartender over. They had long ago cashed out, but he held a few dollars out then anyways.

"For a great night," he said. *And for good luck.* He had not taken a man home in all his time away from Hollie. He darted one last look at Travis and figured he would need it.

They bid the bartender goodbye and Travis followed Nathan out the door.

―――――

"It's very nice. Where'd you get this couch?"

"Surprisingly...IKEA." Nathan draped his coat across the couch's arm and offered a hand for Travis's. The younger man handed it off and smiled.

"Probably cost a fortune."

"IKEA's not that expensive."

"No," said Travis. "But it's not that cheap either."

Nathan was reminded again that Travis was in his first job out of school. Finances were different for the two of them. He shrugged it off and led them further into the house. *It's comfy, too,* he thought as they left the couch behind. He didn't say that, though. He had fluffed the pillows earlier and was thankful it didn't look too slept on.

It was nearing eleven, but Nathan was wide awake. His whole body surged with the type of adrenaline that made him feel like a junkie who had just shot up and moments before thought it'd be fun to double the dose. He fought to keep his face level and his breathing calm as he pointed out a few of the paintings he'd thrifted that now hung in the foyer.

"Come on," he said. "I'll show you upstairs."

Travis had Ubered to the bar, a fact Nathan had not known until they were leaving to come here. *I always uber to bars,* he told him. *Just in case I'm not well enough to drive home.*

Or in case you go home with someone else, Nathan thought. He kept that one to himself, though.

Nathan flicked on the lights at the top of the stairs. He held out his right arm like he was some kind of ringleader and he had just revealed a fabulous display of death-defying acrobats and not an empty hallway that led to a master bedroom on the left, a child's room to the right, and a bathroom straight ahead. Travis laughed and Nathan decided then and there that either Travis was full of absolute shit, or he was already falling head over heels in love with Nathan.

For what it was worth, Nathan hoped it was the latter.

"Snazzy," Travis said.

Nathan chuckled. "It's not much."

Travis stepped ahead into the barren beige hallway. "You should spruce it up. Add some art. Does Tyler draw at all?"

Everything in Nathan went cold. He bit down on his bottom lip. "He's a bit too young for that still."

"Really?" Travis didn't push it though. He did, however, peer into Tyler's room and reach in to flick on the light.

"Oh that's not—" Yellow light bounced from the room into the hall.

"Oops!" Tyler shut the light off again and threw his hands behind his back. "Sorry I thought it was—"

Before he could finish, Nathan stepped up to him though and pushed him against the wall. He leaned in and kissed him there, not sure what was coursing through his body. He felt hot, he felt rugged, his chest felt heavy and light and like it would practically explode if he didn't kiss this man with his uneven lips and quirk of a smile and dark blue eyes that, even as he reached for the wrong light switch, seemed so dangerous, so enticing that already he was addicted.

Travis kissed him back. His hands traveled up Nathan's chest and then he felt cold skin wrap around to the nape of his neck and settle there. He felt Travis's tongue flick against his own, and an audible groan slipped through his lips. Nathan didn't need to breathe; he didn't let himself try. Instead, he pushed deeper into the kiss. He realized as he pushed him harder against the wall that his hand had traveled up Travis's stomach and around his neck now. He pulled him closer to him and felt Travis melt in his hands. It reminded him of the way Hollie had melted the last time they had sex.

He pulled away from Travis for a second just to say, "It's alright."

Travis breathed heavy and said, "It is."

Then he pulled Nathan in for more. His own hand traveled down until Nathan felt him settle on the growing pain in his groin. Another moan escaped him. He felt Travis smile against him.

Then he heard the sound like something slipping against the carpet. He opened his eyes.

Behind him, through the darkness of Tyler's room, he saw a white sheet of paper sitting just outside the shut closet door and shining in the moonlight.

He was suddenly sure it had not been there before.

He closed his eyes and pulled away from Travis. He flicked his eyes open again and smiled down at him. "Give me one second," he said.

Travis looked ready to say something, but Nathan stepped away before he could. He left the bedroom light off and bent down. The paper was warm under his touch as he picked it up and stood again. He unfolded the page with growing dread. His heart beat twice...then a third time before he saw what was on the page. What Tyler had left on the page.

The Lop-Sided man stared back at him.

Light surrounded him. Nathan jumped.

"Whatcha got there?"

He turned to Travis, who stood at the light switch. He walked toward Nathan then and Nathan crumpled the paper. "Just one of Tyler's drawings. He's always leaving them lying around." Except Tyler hadn't been there for days now, and Nathan cleaned up at the end of every visit.

Travis gave him a quizzical look and reached around him. "I thought you said he wasn't into art."

Nathan pulled the paper away from Travis's reaching hand. "Ah, ah," he said in a sing-song voice. Then, he leaned in and kissed Travis again. Soon, the paper was forgotten, and Travis was leaning into him again. Nathan was thankful for the distraction, but his mind was still on the drawing. It had come from the closet; he was suddenly sure. He opened his eyes as he kissed Travis and glanced at the bottom of the door, into the small space between the frame and carpet.

A shadow crossed to the other side of the closet.

Nathan spun the younger man around and slammed him into the closet door. He swore he felt a shudder come from the other side of the closet—almost like someone was pushing to get out—but he pushed harder into Travis and felt the pressure on the other side of the door abate.

It's not really there, he thought. *It can't really be there.*

He reached a hand blindly down the door and settled on the knob. His other hand pushed back on Travis's tight, muscular chest. For such a thin framed guy, he felt big under his shirt. Nathan wanted to see more. He reached around Travis's waist and traced the small of his back. Then, he let his hand lower and drew circles with his palm along the perky perimeter of his ass. It was Travis's turn to moan.

In that moment, Nathan forgot about the door knob and pulled Travis with both hands away from the door. He lifted his chin and broke their kiss. "Follow me."

Travis said nothing but followed close behind as Nathan guided him out the room. He looked back only once as he flicked off Tyler's light. He saw the crumpled ball of paper sitting right outside the closet door. Then, the room went dark, and he led Travis back down the hall and into his bedroom.

Travis didn't leave that room again until morning, when he crawled out from under Nathan's sheets, peeled his clothing off the floor, and walked with Nathan two steps behind to the front door. He told Nathan—with another kiss, this one short, sweet, and somewhat somber—that he would like to hang out again. Nathan told him all he had to do was name a date.

When Travis's Uber picked him up and he was out of sight, Nathan went back upstairs to Tyler's room to pick up the dropped drawing.

Sunlight streamed through the open curtains and revealed the spotless room.

The crumbled paper was gone.

5

It was Travis's idea to install the lock. That Saturday, the two of them went out for drinks a second time. They tried a different bar, and they ordered drinks for one another, trying to find what the other liked most. Travis ordered Nathan a coconut and pineapple drink with enough rum to knock a sailor off the side of his boat. He ordered Travis something called a Hot Girl Summer even though, outside, summer was rapidly fading from view. When they stepped out, Nathan wrapped his jean jacket, which had previously been flung across his lap—for two very different and very practical reasons—around his shoulders, and Travis stepped just a tiny bit closer.

"Back to my place?" he asked.

Travis said he had to get home today. He was getting brunch with friends in the morning and if he showed up late, they would know something was up.

Something was up. It shouldn't have, but that hurt Nathan to think of himself as just *something that was up.* But he agreed and drove Travis home this time, parking outside his apartment building and waiting to turn out of the lot until Travis had unlocked the front door, stepped inside, and let the door swing shut behind him.

The drive home that night was excruciating.

By the time he got home, he decided to approach this whole thing with a more casual flare. Clearly that was what Travis was doing. Nathan stripped and flopped into bed, and as he did, his phone lit up. Travis. *Do you have plans this Wednesday?* Nathan's heart fluttered. He thought now he might.

It was during that date, which took place entirely at Nathan's home and was spent mostly naked and in his bed, that he told Travis about Tyler's night terrors.

"That's what my therapist calls them at least," he said. His head was against the bed's backboard, and his legs were sprawled out. Travis had draped himself across another pillow, laid out on his stomach. His ass was just out of arms reach, but even just looking at it made Nathan start to stir. God, what was happening to him? It was like he was in high school again, impossible urges sparking up at the most inopportune times.

"You don't think that's what they are?" said Travis.

He shrugged. "I don't know. They feel worse. He just...I don't want him to deal with them anymore."

Travis shifted off his stomach and sat at eye level with Nathan. His hand crept across Nathan's bare leg and came dangerously close to his exposed cock. "Have you tried a lock on the door? Like, I know it's a closet, but it could work. Cece had one for years. This one time, me and Irina locked her in the closet while our parents were out on a date. I think she screamed for like an hour before Irina got bored and told me to let her out."

Nathan feigned laughter, but really, he was picturing Tyler screaming for an hour, locked in a closet where he wasn't entirely alone, and his body felt more like a scream was bubbling up.

"She wasn't afraid of the closet after that, though."

"Hmmm." Nathan closed his eyes and let his head loll backwards. As he did, Travis's hand moved again, and warm pleasure spread through Nathan's body. He looked up. "Round two?"

"If you're up for the challenge."

Oh, he was.

Though halfway through round two they stopped; Nathan's heart wasn't in it. He was too busy thinking about what Travis had suggested. When they both laid down again, this time under the covers, with the idea of falling asleep on both their minds, Nathan said, "He comes and visits this weekend."

"That's soon."

"It's been ages."

"Try the lock. I think it might work."

And so, on his lunch break the next day he ran to the Home Depot down the road and asked one of the women who worked there to help him find the right kind. She handed him a brass finished lock pack and asked if he had ever installed one before. He hadn't, so she told him to visit their website for a full video tutorial on what to do, but she gave him a brief tutorial all her own as he stood between the aisles, growing more and more nauseous from the smell of freshly sanded wood.

He got home and remembered very little of what she'd said, so he spent the next hour watching and re-watching the five-minute tutorial, only to fumble the lock as soon as he got it out of the packaging and drop it on the ground. One of the pieces clanged as it hit against the door. The other rolled softly through the carpet and into the empty closet beyond. Between

Tyler's last visit and this one, Nathan had emptied the closet of most of Tyler's things. His clothes and toys and stuffed animals were now strewn across the bedroom floor. He'd re-organize those sometime before Friday night when Tyler would get here. *After,* he thought and reached into the dark closet. He ran his hand along the ground, searching blindly for the missing piece. When he grazed something cold and clammy, and he stumbled back.

What the—

When he looked again it was just an uncovered portion of the hardwood that had been there before the carpet. It had been clammy though, like a human hand. Shudders ran through his body. He reached for the wood again. This time, when he touched it, it felt like wood. Old, probably in need of a dusting, but very much a piece of hardwood floor. His fingers were covered with dust bunnies when he pulled them back. He cleaned them off by rubbing them against the carpet. *Definitely* in need of a dust. *And probably replacement.*

Nathan didn't own the place though, so if the current landlord wanted carpet, they could have carpet. He found the lock piece on the other end of the closet and went back to work putting it together. It took almost another hour until finally the lock was in. He stood up and shut the closet door. Moment of truth. He flicked the lock shut and jiggled the doorknob. It didn't budge. The breath he let out was hot and heavy.

He was ready for Tyler's visit.

They rolled up at quarter to six that Friday night. Hollie got out of the driver's side and lifted her eyebrows to register she saw Nathan, then she went to unbuckle Tyler's car seat. Nathan took a hesitant step forward. "You're later today," he said.

Hollie reappeared from behind the car with Tyler in her arms. He was sliding down, though, and soon both feet were firmly planted on the driveway, and he was running for Nathan. "Daddy, daddy!"

"Hey there buddy." He bent down and hugged Tyler. "Missed ya."

"I missed you too, Daddy."

He stood back up as Hollie walked over. "Sorry," she said. "Work was crazy. Had to stay late again and finish a report for Monday." He noticed then she was dressed in a pair of grey business pants and a matching blazer.

"They work you too hard over there," he said.

"Yeah, well...have to pay the bills somehow."

Since going back to working full time, Hollie had been working as a technical recruiter for a budding startup in the area. She didn't say much about it except that the money was good, and money was what she needed right now, but Nathan could tell by the vacant look in her eyes there were other ways it left her unfulfilled. Where was the Hollie he met in college? With her bright eyes and almost insufferable optimism about the way of the world? Now, there was a dullness to her that made her look sleepy and...and normal.

Her normal eyes darted across Nathan's face, down to his neck, and back up again. Something lit in them, and Nathan held his breath to keep from reaching up to the spot on his neck she was surely looking. The other night, Travis had gotten a bit too fiendish in bed and Nathan had been wearing turtlenecks and collared shirts 24/7 since. Today he forgot himself and wore a crew neck instead. He huffed out a breath.

"How's school going?" he asked.

"It's good!" said Tyler. "The other week, on the playground, Georgie tried to feed Mitchell one of her boogers. He got it smeared all over his mouth, but nothing went inside. He ran away before she could do that."

"Oh, uh, why did she do that?"

"I dunno. She got in trouble for it though."

Hollie let out a little laugh and said, "Mom's helping a lot with pickup."

"I'm glad."

Her mouth pulled taut. "Well, I've gotta get going. Tyler, I'm heading out now."

He ran up and gave his mom a hug as she bent down to his level. For half a second, while they silently embraced in his driveway, Nathan could imagine this was more normal than it was. Hollie was dressed for work, going away on a business trip maybe, but she would be coming back and all would be well with them when she did. The illusion faded as soon as Hollie stood up. Her shark eyes fell on him, and he noticed the smile on her lips never quite reached them.

"Have him back by five on Sunday, okay?"

"You got it," he said.

"And make sure he gets lots of rest. There's something going around school and I don't want him getting sick."

"He'll rest up plenty."

She took a deep breath. "Okay. I trust you."

I trust you. Why had it sounded painful for her to say?

Tyler tugged at his shirt then. "Daddy I'm hungry."

"Just a second, bud. I've got dino nuggets in the oven now," he said. Then he looked up and winked at Hollie. She didn't acknowledge it.

"I'll see you later," she said, and circled back to the driver's side of her cherry colored Chevy Impala. It was odd for this greying version of her to slump into a car that color. That color had been bought by a different version of Hollie at a very different time. Something twisted in his heart. She slouched inside and slammed the door behind her. Tyler and Nathan stood there and waved as she pulled off the driveway and curved down the street.

"So," he said once she'd tapered off completely, "about those dinosaurs?"

"Yeah!!" Tyler raced him inside; Nathan let him win.

The first scream came after midnight. Up until then, their night had been uneventful. After dinner, Tyler had asked to help with the dishes even though he could barely reach the sink. "I do them all the time with Mommy," he said with the kind of fabricated grown up tone only a five year old could muster. Nathan didn't have many dishes to do. They'd used plastic cups, so he held Tyler around the waist and hoisted him up while he washed those. They were still sudsy when Tyler declared them done, and once he was no longer looking, Nathan went back and gave them one more rinse. The plates they'd used were paper, and a simple toss in the garbage took care of the dishes problem. He kept telling himself he'd get real dishes soon. Maybe when Tyler grew up a bit or when he owned a place rather than rented it. Until then, he found difficulty in the justification.

Nathan taught Tyler how to play blackjack after that. The kid got good at it pretty fast, too. Pretty soon he was saying *hit me* like he was some casino-going addict on his fifth drink of an all-night outing. Nathan could practically smell the cigar smoke wafting off him.

"Your grandpa taught me this game when I was your age," said Nathan. "I don't think I was as good at it as you are though."

"Hit me!"

Tyler spread his arms out like eagle's wings as he said it. He looked ready to cheer. Nathan slapped down another card—a 6 of clubs—and the boy did just about explode.

"21 exactly!" said Nathan. "You're rockin' it, bud."

"I love you, Daddy."

And the expression on Tyler's face as he reached for the cards and pulled them into his winning pile—Nathan had told him it wasn't that sort of a game, but he had that go-fish mentality that wouldn't let him see that hoarding his winning cards only made the game go by faster as the stack in Nathan's hands shrank smaller and smaller—well, that expression could've melted any man's heart. Nathan was filled with an overwhelming sense of *this is my kid, I'm responsible for this one*...and he held onto that feeling as Tyler sat back and told him to start again.

"I think that's enough for tonight. It's getting late."

"Nooo, Daddy!"

But Tyler didn't fight long after that. It was later than he usually stayed up; it was always later at Daddy's place. "I'll tell ya a story when I tuck you in, how 'bout that?"

"Yes!"

And so, he did. He didn't remember the story now, but it must've been a good one, or bad one based on your perspective, because Tyler was out like a light only a few minutes in. Nathan gently laid the blanket over him. The nights were growing steadily chilly, so tonight the window was shut and locked tight. A breeze crept across Nathan's neck from somewhere as he walked back to his room, making sure to keep the hallway light on for Tyler. It seemed like he had just laid down himself when he heard the first scream, though he'd probably been asleep for hours. He awoke with that groggy, where-am-I feeling that spread through the whole body but turned the mind especially swampy. It had been so long since Tyler's last visit he almost thought the scream had been part of a very bad, easily forgotten dream.

Then he heard another one.

"Tyler?" He leaped out of bed and ran down the hall. The air was brisk and there was a sense of swiftness to it that made him wonder if Tyler had opened his window in the night. Or maybe something else had.

He got to the boy's room and turned on the lights.

Tyler sat upright in bed, knees to his chin and blanket up to his eyes. He looked like an Egyptian pyramid with a crown of blonde hair and messy, red-rimmed eyes. He'd been crying this time.

"Tyler, Tyler what's wrong?" Nathan went to his bed and knelt.

"It's...he..." Tyler was a sniffling, hiccuping mess.

This was worse than it had been the last time. Nathan glanced at the closet and saw it was still closed. The lock was still turned to shut. Nothing about the thing had budged since Tyler got here this evening.

"Tyler, did you have a bad dream?"

He shook his head and cried deeper. As he cried, the swampy just-waking-up feeling started to flee from

Nathan's head. He stood up and walked to the closet door.

"No!"

"It's okay," he said. "There's nothing wrong. See?" Nathan pulled at the closet door to show how the lock worked.

The door came open with ease.

Nathan jolted back.

The other side of the lock rested on the carpet inside the closet. He glanced at it, then back at the hole in the door where he'd secured the thing just a few days earlier. He reached down and pulled the other side of the lock out of the door. With nothing attached to it, it slid out easily. He turned back to Tyler.

"What happened?"

"He—h-he wanted to talk to me."

"Who did?"

He already knew the answer.

Tyler buried his face in his knees again and he saw for the first time there was a piece of sketch paper next to Tyler's bed. It must've fallen there somewhere in the commotion. As Nathan reached down to pick it up, he half expected a hand to reach out from under the bed and snatch at him. But no, that was being silly. All of this was being silly. There was no Lop-Sided man.

But the lock was broken.

From the inside of the closet.

He picked up the drawing and held it out to Tyler. "Can you tell me what this one is?"

There were two figures sitting across from one another. One was a small, simply drawn boy; the other was the same figure that haunted all of Tyler's drawings. His hat stretched wider now. His eyes looked more hollow. The scribbles that made up his long arm stretched across the ground and rested mere inches from the boy. His other arm was hidden from view. Between them, there was a pile of something. Papers maybe?

"Those are his notes," said Tyler. "He wanted to talk to me."

"What did he want to say?" *Who is he really?*

"I don't know," said Tyler. "He ran down the hall when I screamed."

Ran down the—

Nathan set the drawing down next to Tyler and stepped toward the hallway. "Daddy, no!"

He ignored his son as he peeked from behind the door frame. Light from the bathroom down the hall cascaded onto the ground. In the small triangle of space it showed, Nathan saw a shadow brush past and then vanish into the darkness behind. His fingers tightened on the door frame. *He ran down the hall...*

"Tyler," he whispered. "Come to me."

"Daddy, no." He shook his head and buried his face deeper in his blankets.

"Tyler—" He held out a hand, waiting for him to come grab it. As he did, he kept staring at the end of the hallway. Something stretched in the shadows at the other end of the hall, and Nathan remembered his initial theory that someone snuck in when Tyler left the window open. But that was impossible. The window was shut now. So, unless they'd been in here since then...living in here...waiting...

The edge of a foot found its way into the light. Nathan gasped and the foot slid back. "Tyler!"

Tyler connected with Nathan's hand and relief flooded through him. Tyler was crying again now, but Nathan couldn't find it in him to care. If there was something else in this house, someone who hid in

Tyler's closet and only came out when the boy was here, someone else needed to know. He pulled Tyler out of the room and swooped him into his arms as they ran for the master bedroom. His phone was on the nightstand.

"Grab it!" he told Tyler.

When he did, Nathan ran the two of them downstairs and set Tyler down against the front door. He took the phone and immediately dialed 9-1-1. Upstairs, he heard the creak of a footstep along the floor. He held a hand against the front doorknob as the phone rang.

"Come on...come on..." Fuck why did they take so long to pick up?

Another footstep.

"Daddy...? He's still up there."

A chill ran down Nathan's spine. "I know, bud. I know." *Come on...*

He looked up the stairs then back at the front door. Another ring...then another...For fucks sake someone was upstairs, and they were coming closer. Were they armed? Nathan imagined a long, slender knife brought up from the kitchen. Maybe worse? He shook his head.

And his eyes fell on the alarm system next to the front door. He'd armed it that night, hadn't he? *Yes, yes, I remember that...*He nodded to himself and clung harder to Tyler's hand.

"Cover your ears bud," he said. Then he pocketed his phone and twisted the doorknob. "And get ready to run." He threw open the first door just as the shape of a man appeared at the top of the stairs.

Tyler screamed.

Nathan's vision spun.

And the man vanished down the hall as the screech of the alarm drowned out the world.

In forty minutes, the search was done. Nathan held a sleeping Tyler in his lap as they sat in the front seat of his car, engine off, windows fogged from the lowered temperatures outside. The man who introduced himself as Officer Barnes when he first got to the house, now strolled up to the car and knocked gently on the window. Tyler stirred but didn't wake. It had to be almost 1:30 now. How tired was the boy after all this? Nathan popped the car door open, and Barnes pulled it the rest of the way.

"Coast's clear," he said, voice matter-of-fact.

"Did you find anything?" asked Nathan. *Anyone...*

The officer shook his head. "Nada. Nice bookshelves you got though. The missus a big reader?"

"*I* am."

"Oh, that's cool, that's cool. But no, we didn't find anything." He glanced down at Tyler. "I wanna ask you a few questions though before we head out. That alright?"

"What kind of questions?"

Barnes puffed his chest ever so slightly. "Sir, it's not every day we get a midnight call to the suburbs saying someone's in the house, and then we get there and find no proof of breaking and entering, or of anyone at all. Just wanna know what made you think someone was there?"

Again, another glance at Tyler. Nathan tightened his grip on the boy. "Just...had a feeling, I guess. Thought I heard something." *Footsteps. I heard footsteps, Officer.* He didn't want to tell him about Tyler's night terror. It would only make him sound crazier for believing them in the first place.

"Right. And it's just you here?"

"Usually. My wife and I separated a year or so back."

"Ahh." Nathan didn't like his tone. What did he think he'd suddenly figured out? "New place then?"

"Yes."

"Bigger than the last?"

"A bit."

Officer Barnes leaned deeper onto the side of Nathan's car. "Listen, I'm not much for that mental health mumbo jumbo, but I had this buddy who went through a divorce few years back. He was a wreck for a while. We got him in therapy. It helped a ton."

"I'm already in therapy. That isn't the problem."

"I'm not saying it is." He leaned back from the car. Nathan's tone had a biting quality now. He was suddenly tired. Very tired. "But when you live alone for the first time after awhile, you're bound to hear things. It happens. Phantom footsteps. You see a shadow across the room. That sorta thing."

"I know what I saw."

It was more than a shadow...He pictured the man standing at the top of the stairs. He couldn't remember any details. It had been too dark in there. But he seemed to remember his hat.

"Okay, wicked. And *I know* now that there's nobody else in your house. You're free to go back in."

"Thanks."

Nathan stirred Tyler and helped slide the boy out the driver's side door. As he followed, then lifted Tyler back up (*fuck, when had he gotten so heavy...?*), Officer Barnes came up beside him and said, "By the way, the former Mrs...what's her name?"

He knew by the look in his eye that he was going to call her. By morning, maybe earlier, Hollie would know Nathan had called the police. She would be spamming his phone and trying to get ahold of him. She'd be asking for Tyler back early, maybe permanently. And really, could he blame her?

"Hollie Smart," he said. He hoisted Tyler into a better position. His small head lolled across Nathan's shoulder. "I can give you her number, too."

"Wouldja? You're too kind." His grin was too large for this time of night.

Nathan supplied the number and then said, "Goodnight officer."

He walked back up the drive and closed the door behind him. Minutes later, the cop cars—three of them in total—drove off. Their lights were off, so if you hadn't seen them arrive (*Hell, who am I kidding? Everyone had seen or heard them blare through the sleepy neighborhood at one in the morning on their way directly to the newest occupied house on the block...they must've*), you would've never known they were there in the first place.

When Nathan turned back around, he stood stock-still for a moment and listened. There were no footsteps creeping along upstairs. For tonight, the damage was done.

He brought his son up to his room and tucked him back in. "Sleep tight," he whispered.

Then he went back to his room and got under all his covers. He wasn't sure when he fell asleep, but he remembered waking up twice. The first time because he had to piss; the second because he could've sworn he heard something rattle along the upstairs hall. When he went outside to check it though, whatever had made the noise was gone.

6

"You called the cops while he was there! Nathan, how am I *supposed* to feel about that?"

He didn't have an answer. It was nine the next morning and he had hardly slept a wink. Tyler was still upstairs, probably still tucked in bed, maybe up and coloring in one of the books he brought with him this visit. Nathan was downstairs, pacing around the kitchen island like a vulture in flight. He rammed himself into the corner of the square island at least three times as he walked, and the third time it happened he let out a wince that even Hollie could hear.

"What was that?" she had asked.

"It's nothing," he said. *Nothing but the sound of my heart fucking breaking, Hollie. Just fucking breaking.*

She called around seven while he *had* been sleeping. When at last enough of his grogginess had lifted and his head no longer swam through thick layers of murky fog, there had been thirteen missed calls and twelve text messages. He didn't bother to read the texts before getting out of bed and calling her back. He already knew what this was about.

"I don't know, Hollie," he said. "I just know what I'm telling you. It was a freak thing. Tyler slept through the whole thing. He probably doesn't even remember it."

"That doesn't matter," she said. "You can't do that when there's a little kid around. He's young. Impressionable. Were they carrying guns?"

"I don't know. Probably."

"So then something bad could've really happened."

No, he thought. Something bad could've happened if there had been someone in the house and he hadn't called the cops. *That was when something bad happened, Hollie.* "Nothing did, though," he said.

"And think about the other kids in the neighborhood. Oh God, Nathan, it really is a nice neighborhood."

So why'd ya go and ruin it? The end of her sentence was unspoken, but Nathan heard it loud and fucking clear. It was too early in the morning for this kind of inquisition.

"None of them even saw. It was late. They were asleep."

"Do you know that?"

"No but...Hollie nothing bad happened. It was just a small thing."

She took a breath. "No, not this time." Then, after a pause she added, "I want him back tonight."

Even though he'd known this was coming, hearing it from Hollie turned his blood to stone. He opened his mouth to argue, but all he could choke out was, "I don't..." before conceiving and pivoting to, "Fine. I can do that."

"Thank you. Seven o' clock? I want you to still have the day with him."

"Works for me."

There was dead air at the end of the call. They

used to fill the space with *I love you's* and similar phrasings. Now it just fell silent. "See you then," Nathan said, and hung up the line.

He dropped off Tyler sharply at seven. The boy didn't ask questions about why he was coming home early. Nathan told him he got a call from work and had to do something special for them this weekend, so he needed some extra time, but if Tyler needed the excuse or even bought it, he didn't say. He just sat silently in the back of the car as they drove back to his usual house, got out when they had parked, and ran inside.

Hollie offered Nathan a smile and a wave goodbye. No thanks for bringing him home early. No thanks for trying to keep him safe. Even her smile seemed forced. Whatever, though. He didn't think about it as he drove home that night. He thought instead about Travis. He could have him over earlier than expected. That was a good thing, right? Travis. Travis was a good thing. He thought about the man's sharp jawline and wicked blue eyes. His trim waistline and chiseled chest. The last time he'd been over, Nathan asked him about his workout routine.

He said, "Being young. Oh, and cardio."

Nathan responded, "Fair enough. Some of us don't have that luxury anymore."

But Travis responded by climbing on top of him and kissing him deeply. Nathan shut his eyes and pulled him closer. Now that was luxury.

He thought about him the whole way home, and by the time he was in his driveway and getting out of the car, he had started thinking that maybe all of this was for the best. This was a new chapter for him. And so far, it was a hell of a lot more fun.

His phone dinged when he got inside. He expected Hollie. Maybe Tyler forgot something, or she had a question about why he looked so tired, or what he ate for lunch or dinner. But instead, it was Eliza.

Third time's the charm...D&D wine night tomorrow. You free?

He was free; could be anyways. He'd been free last week too, but he hadn't felt up for a night next door meeting new people and weighing whether or not they would take stock in his life moving forward. Tonight...tonight he felt different. He thought about Hollie's half smile and Tyler's silence on the drive home. He'd been happy to get back to his mom. He liked her better. Saw her home as his. Nathan was just his dad that he visited sometimes now. That much was becoming increasingly clear. Travis wasn't always free —and thank God for that, because as fun as it would be, the chafing would be unbearable—and, Nathan wasn't sure how long it would serve him to have Travis be the only person around him who wasn't tainted by a life gone by.

New chapter, he thought again, and then texted her back.

I'll bring a bottle of Riesling. See you there.

Eliza's husband answered the door when he knocked.

"Nathan! Good to see ya! Come in, come in." He stepped aside and let Nathan in. "Eliza's just upstairs freshening up. Maryanne and Penny are already here. They're in the kitchen."

"Thanks," Nathan said with a smile.

Ethan Shepherd was a large man, who stood at well over six feet and whose belly protruded like that of a woman in her second trimester; his baby blue T-shirt jutting up and revealing the smallest sliver of bare skin at the bottom of his torso. He wore wire rimmed glasses and had a head full of thick, deep brown hair. His lips were the kind of full that almost seemed to quiver just standing there, but then when they pulled into a smile they became normally proportioned to his face. Nathan looked up at the man to thank him for holding the door, and suddenly he felt very short. *I'm 5'11",* he thought.

The back of Ethan's shirt was decorated with an intercrossing of swords and a word written in symbols Nathan didn't recognize. He thought about asking what it said, but by that time they were already in the kitchen, and Ethan was passing him off with another round of introductions.

He knew the two women in the kitchen only through brief glances. Maryanne lived a few blocks over and usually attended the block parties the neighborhood sometimes threw. She was a Latina woman who was at least a head shorter than everyone else in the kitchen. She twirled a glass of wine in her hands and tucked a highlighted strand of hair behind her ear as she stepped forward to greet him. "Glad you could make it." She wrapped him in a hug while the other woman, Penny, stood patiently behind. When Maryanne pulled apart, Penny stepped forward. Her hair was that ashy sort of brown that looked almost to be greying. Both women were probably approaching forty, but there was a youthful buzz about the room. When Penny hugged him, she slipped the bottle of Riesling out of his hands.

"I'll fridge this," she said. "Chilled white is the only way to go."

"Oh absolutely," said Maryanne. "What brand is it?"

"It's just from Target," said Nathan. He hadn't checked the brand before purchasing. It had been $7.99. That was really all he'd cared about.

"Lovely." Penny stuffed it in the fridge and as she did, Ethan asked if she could pass him a few more of the beers stuffed in the back.

"You don't want one, do you, Nathan?"

"What? No, no, it's fine."

Ethan nodded and took the two beers Penny handed him. "I'll be in the basement," he said. "When the others show let 'em know where to find me."

"You got it," said Maryanne. When he was gone she turned to Penny. "Here, get Nathan something to drink. You like white or red?"

"I mean, I brought white."

"Perfect, so we'll start with red."

"Start? No, I work tomorrow. I can't drink too much."

"Oh please," she said. "We all work tomorrow. That's why we drink this much."

Eliza came down the stairs as Penny was pouring the drinks. Her hair was slightly damp, and she was dressed in black sweatpants and a tight fitted blue shirt. She looked like a video vixen from a 90s hip hop video if the vixen had moved to the suburbs, and grown up by a good five, six, seven years. Penny and Maryanne nodded at her as she joined them and then refilled their own glasses first. A bit of the red sloshed outside of Penny's as she poured. How much had she had before Nathan got here? Then, she poured a glass for each of the others. As she did, Eliza pulled Nathan into a brief side hug. "Glad you made it."

"Me too."

The four of them clinked their glasses and moved to the living room. Unlike in his own house where the living room was directly across from the kitchen, here it was the first room to the left of the front door. The window was still open, and Nathan saw a duo of scootering kids race by in the growing dimness. He noticed neither of them were wearing helmets—the kind of thing you only notice once you've got a kid of your own to worry about. Next to the window was a little mantel with framed photos lining the top. Photos of Eliza and Ethan in college, probably when they met, when they first moved in together (if all the moving boxes in one of them were to be believed), and so on. He reached out and straightened one of them. A singular photo of Eliza in a bathing suit with slicked back hair and a medal around her neck.

"Told ya I was an athlete," she said.

He jumped. "You said it was soccer, though." He turned and faced the picture to her, as if she didn't already know what it looked like.

"And swim," she said. "That stopped first though. I couldn't do the mornings once winter hit. Have you ever gotten into a swimsuit while it's twenty degrees out? It's not natural, I tell ya."

"No, I haven't." He replaced the photo and Eliza reached across his body for the one next to it. She pulled it from the mantel and held it up.

"Here's a soccer one."

It was more than just a soccer one. In the picture, Eliza had clearly just finished a game, and big, strong Ethan had wrapped her in her arms and was kissing her. Her ponytail hung straight down and his hand was on her leg. It made Nathan hot to look at it too long. There was so much passion burning off the image. He darted his eyes southward and nodded. "I'll say. When was this?"

"College. Early college. Probably a week or so after meeting Ethan. My friend Gena snapped it when we weren't looking."

"It's a great photo."

Nathan had those kinds of photos with Hollie, where happiness was tangible, and the moment being captured locked the rest of the world out. He had those photos somewhere in one of the boxes he hadn't unpacked since the move. They would stay tucked in there; it was better off that way.

The rest of the photos lacked the same intimacy. A staged wedding photo that looked happy, but clearly something was missing. *I also have* those *photos,* Nathan thought. Next to the wedding photo was another staged one of the two of them sitting in the sand. Eliza noticed where his gaze had fallen.

"Honeymoon photoshoot."

"Oh," he said. "Kinda, uh, tame for a honeymoon."

She laughed. "My mom paid for it. It was like an early Christmas present. We were in the Bahamas, and she hired some random guy to come wake us up early in the morning for a dawn shoot. All we had to do was doll up and show up. When I gave her a framed copy of the photoset, she started to cry."

"Geez."

"Yeah. Almost like it wasn't her idea in the first place." Eliza shook her head and dusted a finger across the top of the frame. If you asked him, she looked uncomfortable in the photo. Knowing it was so early in the morning made sense, and they'd probably been up late the previous night. It was their honeymoon after all...

"My brother never got married," said Eliza, turning to Nathan now. "He's in his forties and still flying solo. I'm pretty sure she hates it, so I'm her favorite by default."

"Ladies...?" Maryanne stepped up behind them and Nathan felt a hand fall onto his shoulder. "Care to share with the class?"

"I was just showing Nathan some pictures," Eliza said.

"Yeah, never been here before."

"Never?" asked Penny. She was still sitting on the couch, and pretty soon the rest of them all joined her over there. Nathan sat next to Eliza while the other two sat on the other side. The couch was an L shape with an ottoman in the middle. He waited until at least one of the other girls kicked their feet up to settle his own onto the ottoman, and once he did, he nuzzled back into the couch and found himself growing steadily comfortable.

"It's nice here," he said unprompted then. "Way nicer than my place."

"You live next door. How different can it be?" asked Eliza.

I don't know. What lives in your closets?

"It's a lot more grey...I like the brown and green." The couch was a deep tan color that went well with the darker brown tones of the rest of the room. There was art on the wall behind him of a forest that added a pop of green on one end, and then various potted plants tied the color into the rest of the room.

"Thanks. Ethan loves plants."

"You get good light, I'm sure."

She nodded, and then the conversation moved to

what sort of planting Penny had done as of late. Apparently, her green thumb knew no bounds. Pretty soon, Ethan found himself becoming the same sort of wallflower his college friends had been used to. Penny was still talking, and he was reaching for the bottle of red to refill his glass when the doorbell rang again. They were expecting two more people—Helen from two streets over and Phoebe, her friend from out of town.

"Phoebe's great," said Maryanne to Nathan as Eliza got the door. "She visits all the time. She's over on the west side of the state now." She set her glass down and held up her palm in the shape of the Michigan map. "Right around here..."

She circled the southwestern point on her palm and Nathan awed like he knew where that was on the map. He had this theory that most Michiganders knew about the shape of their map, but not exactly where they were pointing to each time.

Introductions were made over another cheers. Helen's husband went downstairs and both women filled out the few remaining spots on the couches. By now, Nathan had a healthy buzz and the overwhelming fear of coming over tonight had started to fizzle. He let the evening envelop him and pretty soon he was talking and laughing along with the women almost like he belonged.

"So, are you seeing anyone, Nathan?" asked Penny.

An hour had to have passed since they all got there. Nathan was on his third glass of wine and had been nursing it steadily. Someone had popped open the Riesling, and now half the bottle was gone. From downstairs, he heard the sudden shouts of the four men. In a world gone by, he would've been expected to be down there with the other husbands. Hollie would be up here in his stead, laughing and drinking and being merry.

He thought maybe he liked it more up here.

"Am I what?" he asked.

"Seeing anyone," Penny repeated.

"I—" Travis came budding to mind, "I guess so, yeah kinda, I am."

Suddenly the room zoomed in on him. Eliza contorted her body to face him. Maryanne sat down in the free spot on his right; Phoebe sat on the couch's arm next to her. The others stayed where they were, but they side conversations died, and Nathan felt the rush of five pairs of eyes on him all at once.

"Uh...his name's Travis?"

"Ooh!" said Helen. "He sounds handsome."

I haven't said anything about him.

"Uh yeah, it's nothing official now though. We've just been hanging out." They kept staring at him, eyes sparkly and mouths pursed as they sipped their wines. What more did they want him to say? *We met on an app you all know nothing about. He's younger than me, and sometimes I feel weird about that even though Landry tells me it's perfectly normal. I don't think it's going anywhere serious, but I sort of wish it would. I'm the top, since you all seem so damn curious...*

He sipped his wine and waited for someone else to break the tension.

"I for one think it's great," said Eliza. "It's harder to meet someone the older you get."

"Wow," he said, "thanks."

Eliza flashed him a gentle smile and shrugged.

"Please. And you would know this how?" asked Penny. "Looking for a side-piece, Shepherd?"

"If I was, you wouldn't be able to call me Shepherd

anymore." Penny said. "But no, I feel like it is. Especially with a kid in the mix."

"Ugh, no kidding." Phoebe stood up and walked back to the ottoman where she'd been planted before. She rattled on about her three-year-old daughter and how happy she was to have her in her life, but how much of a wrench it threw into the dating world. "She's just always another person to think about. I can't go on a date and think about whether or not this person makes me happy without also worrying they won't make her happy." Helen patted her friend's thigh and Nathan nodded along as she spoke.

"Does she live full time with you?" he asked.

She turned to him. "Mostly. She's with her dad some holidays. We don't talk a lot really. Things didn't end well. You have a son, right?"

"Tyler," he nodded. "He's almost six now."

The room awed accordingly.

"Does he stay with you?" Phoebe asked.

He shook his head. "Just weekends. Sometimes."

"That's still hard though. I mean, some guys don't even wanna touch you if you've got a kid. Damaged goods or whatever they call us."

Nathan nodded. He didn't date much, but up until now he'd kept Tyler completely out of the picture. Most of the guys he met were from Grindr, and dating wasn't always top of mind there. A few found out he had a kid if they stuck around long enough for a conversation, but he usually didn't hear from those ones after. It didn't help that they were all a bit younger, like Travis.

I don't mean to date younger, he'd told Landry when finally, he'd been brave enough to bring it up. *It just happens.*

As it should, she'd responded. *You didn't get to date*

men in college and your early twenties. It makes sense you're seeking them out now.

He didn't know what that meant though moving forward. Did that fade? Or was he always going to be seeking them out? He'd seen those profiles online of men in their fifties and beyond *looking for younger only*...or however they chose to phrase it on any given day. What if he became something like that?

Then he thought about Travis again and sipped his wine. Maybe something would work out before then.

The conversation split then, and Eliza asked, "did you drop Tyler off today?"

His breath caught in his throat. "Yesterday. There was an...an accident on Friday. Had to get him home early"

He searched her face for any sign that she'd seen the cop cars pull up. She must've been asleep, because nothing registered in her face. *Good*, he thought. But she kept glancing at him as the night went on, and the more he drank, the less sure he was that the vacant expression in her face was because she didn't know. There was an intention behind the blank stare that he didn't like.

When the night was winding down and the campaign session had ended (Nathan was blissfully unaware of how D&D worked, and he intended for it to stay that way; the way all the men came back upstairs like they'd been through a literal battle left him convinced whatever they were doing was not for him), Eliza pulled Nathan aside.

"I'm glad you came tonight," he said.

"Yeah, me too. Thanks for the, uh, many invites."

She smiled. "'Course. It's fun. You're always welcome. I…figured you might need some company this week."

Her face gave her away. "You saw them."

"Hard to miss the lights," she said. "Ethan slept through it. I just want to know if everything's okay."

"More than okay," he said. "False alarm. Paranoid dad."

"You sure?"

He nodded, though his whole body tightened. "Totally."

"Okay. Well, I'm glad. And if you ever need some extra help…I mean, I know nothing firsthand but I'm sure it can get hard constantly reintroducing a kid to your life. My parents separated when I was in middle school and sometimes, I wonder how they did it. As a kid it was so seamless, but…" she shook her head.

"I don't know if it's always so seamless to Tyler," he said.

"Give the kid some credit. He's got a choice in the matter too, right? He keeps coming back to you. If it wasn't so seamless, wouldn't he just stop choosing that?"

"I guess so."

He was the last one out the door that night. His bottle of Reisling had been finished, but he took the bottle back to recycle at his place. When he waved Eliza and Ethan goodnight, he thought again about what she'd told him. How much of a choice did Tyler really have? What would he choose if the choice was only his? He opened his front door and decidedly pushed the thought to the back of his mind. That didn't matter right now. He was coming back to him as long as he didn't screw this thing up.

The first place he went once the door was locked was Tyler's room. Earlier in the day he had reinstalled the closet lock; he wanted to make sure it was still intact.

When he rounded the corner, the closet door was closed.

He jiggled the knob and found it shut tight. He breathed easier. Just a freak accident, he told himself. Or what had he called it? Paranoid dad...Yeah, that was it. Surely. Then, wine drunk and feeling lighter for the first time in a few days, he went to his own room and fell asleep.

It was in the morning he found the closet door ajar and the lock broken in two. He didn't know it, but something else broke that morning—in his mind this time—but he carried on like everything was fine because that was the expectation.

Another broken lock...

The closet door ajar...

Nathan was at his desk in the study and buried his head in his hands. He could've sighed away the world's weight, but his breath got caught in his throat. He let it out in little bursts and shook his head.

Everything was *not* fine.

OCTOBER

7

Nathan had his chair pulled sidelong with Landry's at his session the next day. Papers were sprawled out across their laps, and Nathan pointed at one on the far side of Landry's leg. Her fingers caressed the bottom of it. "And look at that!" he said. "What does that look like?"

At first, Landry made a show of pulling the paper closer. Then, she lowered it and let out a deep sigh. Nathan heard how crazy he must sound in the low notes of that breathy exultation. "It's just more scribbles, Nathan."

He grabbed the paper and held it up. They had been at this for almost a full thirty minutes, the first thirty minutes of his last session before he would have to renew his yearly plan with Landry to keep seeing her. This marked the end of his first year, and she had intended this session to be a wrap-up. She'd said as much when he walked in. *Nathan, congrats on one year. That's a huge step. How have you been feeling about it?* But quickly he had hijacked the meeting and led Landry in a direction she had been ill prepared to embark in. *I want a second opinion on all this,* he told her.

"It's the lock. I put a lock on the door and still, nothing."

The drawing showed the closet door front on. At first, it looked like just a closet. A rectangle made of sharp edges and thin lines with a handle and a little X for a closed lock in the center. But underneath the door, Tyler had drawn two shadowy circles that jutted out ever so slightly. They were easy to miss, but Nathan hadn't missed them.

"And those are feet," he told Landry. "He drew *feet* under the locked door."

"Kid's draw lots of things."

"Not like this."

"No, not always like this. Nathan, if you're concerned about your son's mental health, I would be happy to search my contacts and see if I can refer you to a child psychiatrist who—"

"I'm not concerned about his mental health. I'm concerned for his safety."

Landry's eyes narrowed. "And why is he unsafe, Nathan?"

"Because—" The rest of the words fell out on his lips. Even he knew better than to tell her about the Lop-Sided man and about what he thought he saw or heard on the nights Tyler was visiting.

Landry brushed the drawings aside and stood. The tea kettle she'd brewed before his session sat on a hot plate across the room. She went to it and gently poured them each a cup of tea. She handed one to Nathan. "Thanks." The scent of peppermint swirled in his nostrils.

"Nathan, how has it been raising Tyler all alone?"

"I don't raise him alone," he said. "He's with Hollie most the time."

"Right. But when he's with you."

"It's fine. Always has been. He's a good kid."

Landry took a long, drawn-out sip of her tea. She puckered, probably from the heat. "I wonder though if maybe this whole...split household thing is causing you more turmoil than it needs to."

"What do you mean?"

She sat again and took a second sip. The pucker smoothed out quicker this time. It reminded him of his whiskey count. It always went down smoother the more sips you took. "You say Tyler is unsafe at your house. You've told me he's having night terrors and screaming through most of his visits."

"Only after dark."

She nodded. "And then you bring in...these...and, well, Nathan I'm not sure what else to think. Raising a child is hard work. I have two kids myself and without my husband to help along the way, I don't know what I would've done. Probably lost all my hair. Probably fled the country. Johnny and Ava are fine now. They're grown. Ava's graduating high school this year and Johnny is almost through college. Things are still hard, but different now. When they're young...Well, think of it this way. Nowadays, you worry enough for two. Tyler is a child. He doesn't know what's right and what's wrong. Similarly, he can't always tell when he's safe and when he isn't. Kids are notorious for getting up to things they shouldn't. It's our job as parents to keep them safe as they grow. And you're doing what seems like a wonderful job of that, but you're worried. You're worried he might run into something unsafe around every corner, and that is perfectly normal. It's just you. There is no co-parent to offset some of the worry. When you do mention your ex-wife in our sessions, it's very brief. Curt, I'd say. You can't bear the weight of raising Tyler all yourself. It's just too much.

So." She took a deep breath. "I am suggesting we *up* our scheduled visits to twice a week in the new year. I have a few more openings, and I think it would help for you to talk through these fears more than once a week. How does that sound?"

The room went silent. While she rattled on, Nathan's head started spinning. He stared down at Tyler's disturbed drawings strewn across his lap, on the floor, tucked in his back pocket, and shook his head lightly. *I'm not stressed. Not over nothing.*

"That's—that's not it," he said. That morning the lock had been broken clean in half. The door had been opened. It hadn't been the night before.

Landry sighed. "Nathan. Trust me."

His eyes fell on the drawing he found poking out from under Tyler's bed that morning. The closet door was clear in this one. The lock on its knob was even clearer. Yet still the door was ajar, and something dark and spindly was crawling out. Or, rather, crawling back in. The Lop-Sided man was on all fours, and in his mouth looked to be a round and bulbous thing, a head. Dark pen stains leaked from the head, trailing across the carpet in immaculate detail. Where the trail of blood began, a body lay motionless. Nathan's whole body tightened as he pictured Tyler in the drawn body's stead. His fist crinkled the drawing, and he took a sharp intake of breath.

"No," he said. "No, that's alright." He stood suddenly. Pages flew off his lap and he bent over to collect them.

"Nathan—"

"This has been a wonderful experience," he said, not meeting her eyes as he gathered Tyler's creations. *He drew these*, he thought. *He saw these in his mind. He knows something...* "But I can't keep doing this."

"Nathan please just sit—"

"I will not be upping our sessions. Thank you so much, but I think it's time I go."

"We have to choose a slot for you in the new year then."

"No that's quite alright." He picked up the last drawing. This one was almost entirely drawn out with black, streaky pen marks. Two white eyes glared back at him, slanted up top and jagged at the bottom. He balled it into a fist. "I think it's best if I take Tyler and his drawings and don't come back."

"Nathan!"

"Have a good day, Dr. Landry."

"Nathan!"

He opened the door and squinted against the light. His papers slid around in his arms. He didn't bother to collect the few that fell. *Let them stay*, he thought. Let them be a reminder that something was hiding in his closet. Something was trying to get his son.

I have to stop it—

I have to stop it—

He slammed the door behind him and cut off Landry's last frantic call out to him.

He threw the drawings across the counter when he walked back into his house. Then, he doubled over and put his forehead against the cool granite. He shut his eyes and tried not to think about Landry. Instead, he thought about Travis. He should invite him over. They could have a drink and watch that movie Travis was trying to get him to see. They wouldn't pay attention, but Nathan would appreciate having it on in the background.

His pocket buzzed.

He grabbed his phone and slid a finger across the screen to pick up. His head was still reeling; so much so he hardly noticed Hollie's name on the caller ID. "Babe, I can't talk right now. I'm uh cleaning up and—" He stopped, realized what he'd said.

Babe.

He coughed. "Hollie," he said. His voice became frantic. "*Hollie*, I can't talk."

She remained silent a moment longer. He thought for a second maybe she wasn't there at all, and it had been nothing more than a butt dial. Then she said, "You're at home?"

He looked up. "Yes?"

"Okay." She let out a long breath. "Your therapist called."

"I—why did she call you?"

"I'm still your emergency contact," said Hollie. "She said you stormed out and she wanted to make sure you got home safe." A long pause. "She also said you discontinued your meetings with her."

"I—er, yes. I did."

"Why?"

The question was almost laughable. Why, she asked? Why? *Why, dear Hollie. Because instead of listening to what was happening and attempting to understand, she tried to sign me up for more sessions. Like talking about it would help more. Like Tyler's drawings and the noises in the closet and the footsteps and the broken lock were all just things in his mind. As if Tyler slept perfectly and would be even better if only he signed up for even more sessions. Give me more money, Nathan. You'll feel so much better after that. Here, I'll even connect you with a child psychiatrist. They'll charge extra but I'll get a solid com-*

mission and we'll all live happily ever after. Isn't that right, Nathan? Nathan? Nathan?

"Nathan!"

He realized Hollie was shouting at him.

"What? What?"

Her breath came sharp and static over the phone. "What's going on with you? Is everything okay?"

"I. Yes, perfectly. Why do you—?"

"Because you called the cops this weekend over nothing. You stormed out of therapy. You told her you'd stop going. Whenever Tyler comes back from you, he sleeps deeper and longer than ever. Nathan, something is up. Not to mention last time I saw you, I saw you had...you had..."

His neck.

"That's none of your business," he said.

"Yes it is! It is when you're doing *that* instead of hanging out with Tyler on the weekends he comes over."

"You think that's what I'm doing? Going clubbing and making out with guys instead of spending time with my son?"

She stopped short. "I didn't say anything about them being guys." She took another breath and said, "I don't care what you're doing. You have a life to live now. I get that. I just...if you aren't ready to have Tyler be a big part of it yet, that's fine. He'll understand. And so will I."

Something was not computing. There was no way he was actually hearing her say what he thought she was saying. He paced away from the kitchen—he left the drawings out—and flopped onto the couch. He shook his head and held the phone out in front of him. He put Hollie on speaker phone when he realized she was still trying to talk to him.

"—and it doesn't have to be forever," she said. "I just want what's best for Tyler and what's best for you. And if this arrangement isn't working then—I mean... I know you're further away now. Life is different than it was last year. I get it."

"No!"

She stopped and breathed for a second. He matched his own breaths to hers and tried to clear the fog rising in his mind. "No," he repeated. "That's not it. I just...I'm just still getting settled here."

"Well," she said. "Do you need help?"

"No." His voice was flakey and croissant like. He could barely hear it himself. "No that's okay," he said with more assurance. "I just, I just want to do right by him. And by you." He lifted his chin and turned to the stairs leading up. "Tyler can still come next weekend. I'll make sure he sleeps well. Besides," he took a sharp breath, "I wanted to do something fun for his birthday next month."

Hollie didn't answer for some time. Nathan checked twice to make sure the call hadn't been disconnected before she finally said, "Okay. That's fine. But if you need anything—"

"I will let you know."

And that was that. They ended their call shortly after and Nathan sat there for God knows how long before standing from the couch, gathering up Tyler's drawings into a neat pile, and walking up the stairs to replace them in the nightstand drawer. He kept his eyes on the closet as he did, and kept his ears perked to the sound of something behind there. When he heard nothing for long enough, it was almost possible to convince himself he had imagined the whole thing. No, that's not possible. He had felt the rattle. He had seen the shadow pass beneath. He looked down now and saw nothing in the darkness on the other side of the closet.

It's only ever at night, though.

Yes, that was it.

Nathan sunk down onto Tyler's bed. The frame creaked under his weight. Something echoed the sound from the other side of the room. *No, no there was nothing. And yet...*Nathan shifted on the bed. Waited for another echo. But nothing came. His eyes were glued to the closet. The knob didn't rattle. The light didn't flicker on. The wood didn't bend or shake from an attempt to get out. He looked out the window. The sun crept lower on the horizon and the sky was blooming with orange light. Then, he looked out the bedroom and thought about the closet down the hall. There was a baseball bat in there he hadn't touched since moving in. If he could bring that with him...right as the moon was growing full...

He got up, listened for another echo that didn't come, and then left Tyler's bedroom. A moment later he returned, baseball bat in hand. When he sat down again on the bed, something in him felt safer. He felt suddenly ready.

You worry enough for two, Landry had said.

I just want what's best for Tyler, Hollie had said.

So do I, he thought. And so, as the sun sank lower in the ever-darkening sky, Nathan sat and waited for a monster to rattle out of the closet.

Somewhere in the waiting, he fell asleep.

When he woke again, the room was completely dark aside from the glow of a porch light next door and the solid moon up above. The baseball bat had slipped out of his hands and now rested next to the bed. The pillow was crushed under his back. The sheets were undisturbed. He sat up slowly and saw his phone on top of the nightstand. It lit up with a new message from Travis. He would respond to that later. Probably another invite to hang out soon.

The sound of scratching rose in the silence.

He turned to the closet door which was still locked. The scratching grew louder as he focused. It sounded like a branch hitting lightly against the side of a house, or a piece of worn-down chalk drawn against a dirtied chalkboard. And then, as quickly as it arrived...

It stopped.

The room went uncomfortably silent.

Nathan heard his own pulse deafeningly loud in his ears. For a long moment, he didn't breathe. To let out any air in the deafening silence seemed wrong. Then, when he couldn't hold back anymore and his lungs caught fire with the tension against them, he exploded out, and the gasp that escaped him felt loud enough to wake the neighbors. He kept his eyes on the closet.

From inside, a floorboard creaked.

His body went rigid.

The doorknob twisted in the dark, and Nathan bent down and reached for the baseball bat. He shifted onto his stomach and the bed lurched beneath him. He kept his eyes on the turning knob. The door creaked open then, just the tiniest sliver of even darker night shone through from the other side. He fingered for the bat, but it was just inches out of reach. *Fuck*, he breathed. The door opened further. He scooted closer on the bed and wrapped a hand around the wood. He sat up with the bat in front of him as the door slid further open.

From the other side, he saw a pair of glowing yellow eyes sitting low in the shadows.

He wasn't sure if he was still breathing now.

Naaaathaaaannn...

The voice echoed through his head, but the room stayed perfectly silent. His hands went numb against the baseball bat. He tried to stand up, but his legs were fast asleep. Pins and needles poked from under his skin and fought to get out. His lungs collapsed and breath sputtered out.

A set of long, claw-like fingers crept around the frame of the door.

Where is he Naaaaathaaaann...

This time, his voice clogged up his windpipe. He coughed and said, "Who?"

He knew who though, and the Lop-Sided man didn't bother to tell him.

He just crept further out of the closet until the inky black of his skin fell through the closet and onto the carpet before him. His shorter arm stayed on the door frame while his longer one lugged across the floor. His eyes glowed from beneath a wide brimmed hat made entirely of shadow. *He* was made entirely of shadow. Like he was scribbled straight from one of Tyler's drawings, the man lumbered forward.

"Stah-stop," Nathan stuttered. "Don't m-m-move." He held his baseball bat out but knew suddenly it wouldn't do anything. The Lop-Sided man could do as he pleased. This was his domain as much as it was Nathan's. It was after dark. The dark belonged to him.

Naaaathaaaaannn...

He twisted his hands around the bat and finally stood up. *Just one swing*, he told himself. *One good*

swing and it'll all be done. All of this will finally be over.
He tried to swing but his arms didn't move. His legs
still felt like jelly. His shoulders were like rocks. He felt
encased in molasses with how slow he was. The Lop-
Sided man tilted his head up, and Nathan saw sharp,
jagged teeth glisten in the moonlight.

Outside, the porch light blinked out.

He was entirely alone.

Now—do it...Now!

He went to swing.

Naaaaathaaaannn...

The bat came down just as Nathan woke up.

"Nathan!"

The bat crunched against the nightstand. The
force rattled his shoulder blades and sent him stumbling backwards. He missed his phone by inches.

"Nathan!"

He turned around.

A woman stood in the doorway.

"Eliza?" Nathan stuttered. He looked from her to
the window where her porch light had been on a few
seconds ago, then back to her. "What are you...what
are you doing here?"

"I heard you scream," she said. "A—it was a few
times. I didn't know what was happening, so I thought
I'd knock on your door. It was already open."

Already open? He thought about the closet door's
lock, broken in two.

"I...I screamed?"

Eliza looked at the bat in his hands. Nathan
dropped it and felt the carpet rattle under foot. For
some reason he looked toward the closet. It was
closed. The lock was turned shut.

"A few times," she repeated. "Is everything
alright?"

Nathan blinked a few times before answering. "I think...I think I fell asleep."

And Eliza nodded like that said everything. "Night terrors?" Her voice sounded oddly like Langly's then. "Don't worry, I get them too. I don't always —I mean..." she looked at the nightstand again. Nathan did too, and realized he would have to get a new one before Tyler visited again. The thing was still standing, but the top looked like the Grand Canyon had suddenly formed down the center, and the splinters on all sides were fallen pieces of stone and slate. "I don't always break things when I do but...I get it."

They walked downstairs together where Nathan sat on the couch and rubbed his temples and Eliza, with instruction from Nathan, made him a glass of warm milk.

"You sure you don't need anything else?" she asked as she handed off the glass. It was warm to the touch and Nathan gratefully wrapped both palms around it. He shook his head, but Eliza hovered a moment longer. They checked the front door together. The lock was still intact, just open.

"I won't make a habit of breaking and entering anymore," she joked.

"I think this time we can make an exception."

She turned back to him. God, he must've looked pathetic. His body felt weak and achy all over. What kind of a dream could do that? *It's not a dream*, he thought. *It never was a dream.*

Nightmare, he corrected.

Real life...it was real life.

No.

He offered her a weak smile and thanked her again for coming. "Sorry I couldn't give you the grand tour."

It wasn't lost on him that this was her first time being inside his place.

"It's alright. Next time," she said.

He nodded. "I have to get some real sleep now, I think," he said.

"I hear ya. My dad used to say this thing where if you sleep bad on a Monday the rest of the week's gonna be real shit."

He lifted his warm milk. "Here's to hoping he's wrong then."

She smiled again and headed out. He closed the door behind her and made sure again that it was locked. He finished his milk and (after checking the front door was locked two more times) went back up to Tyler's room.

The room was perfectly still when he got there. He picked up the baseball bat and his phone and told himself tomorrow he'd head to IKEA for a new nightstand. Unless Travis had a better idea. He checked his messages and saw two from him. The first was just checking on him after therapy was done. The second was a link to a video with the accompanying text *made me think of you.*

Nathan smiled before he even clicked on the video. He pocketed his phone and looked again at the silent closet. He closed his eyes and saw the Lop-Sided man creeping out again. When he opened them though, there was nothing.

There was no Lop-Sided man, he told himself as he walked out. "Nothing's in there," he said. "Nothing."

He turned out the light as he left, and the room stayed nearly silent behind him.

Nearly.

8

H e kept Tyler's door closed the rest of the week. Sometimes, only at night, he could've sworn he heard something knocking on the other side of that door, something that was free to roam and explore without interruption now. Others he heard nothing. He did not call Dr. Landry. He did not call Hollie. There was one time *she* called *him*, but it was only to ask if he could pick Tyler up from school that Friday and bring him back to her place. He couldn't. There was a Halloween work event that was technically optional, but Nathan's work had been slipping and his boss had started noticing.

I just want to make sure everything is alright, he said to him. *You seem distracted in our meetings. And it's not like you to forget important things.*

Except it was becoming exactly like him to forget important things.

He never went back to Eliza's D&D party—not because he didn't want to go, but because he usually forgot. He still saw Travis on occasion, but the constant texts they once shared were starting to dwindle. He wasn't sure if that was on him or Travis. Sometimes the girls from D&D would text, mostly Penny, who, as far as Nathan was concerned, seemed almost lonelier than him. She was just comfortable with the loneliness. Sometimes Phoebe would send pictures of her daughter though, and that would make Nathan smile. Usually, he could keep the bitter feeling about her seeing her kid full-time at bay, too. Usually.

Even without it, the only person he thought about consistently was Tyler.

Tyler, who was a world away and, other than a few calls throughout the weeks, seemed ready to stay there. He started each call with an, 'I miss you,' and ended each one with, 'I love you.' But how far did missing and loving really go when the person you missed and loved wasn't good at caring for you right?

On the morning of October 30th, Nathan picked up his phone and made the call.

"Hello? Nathan—what's up?"

Hollie knew he never called first. It had been almost three full weeks since the police incident and in that time he had not initiated once. She never told him this, but sometimes it made her think back to the college days, when they were first getting together, how anxious she'd been talking to friends about him because of how rarely he took the initiative. *"There's no way he's into me like that,"* she said. *"If he was, he'd show it. I mean...he does show it, but wouldn't he call me? Or text me? Or something? Yeah...I guess he schedules dates, and he calls them dates which is like really really big, but still..."*

There had been something she loved about that time. The chase was half the fun of the loving relationship to come. Nathan also remembered that time fondly, though he never knew how little direct interest he showed.

Maybe he was always just too in his head.

"Hey," he said, then paused.

"Do you wanna talk to Tyler? I can get him. He's upstairs and—"

"No no, that's okay. I, uh wanted to talk to you."

"Oh." Another pause. "Okay."

Nathan, who had moments ago been circling his island, now stood against the cold of his refrigerator; he leaned his head back and closed his eyes. A sob threatened at the base of his throat. He held it back.

"I think maybe you're right."

"I'm right?" She was confused; he knew she was confused.

"About Tyler. Him coming here. Maybe it shouldn't happen."

"Nathan what—"

"Nothing happened," he stopped her. "I just can't stop thinking that you're right."

He felt stupid to lie. Of course something happened. Something was always happening. Up the stairs, down the hall, through the closet, something was always forming and morphing and fighting to get out. But he couldn't tell her that. He couldn't tell her why Tyler shouldn't come anymore. He had tried to tell Landry; she had looked at him like a fool. He had talked to Travis about it, but he'd laughed it off and just asked to see the closet for himself.

See it? See it? You can't see it, Travis. I care about you too much to let that happen! And now that I've denied you, you're gonna leave. Leave like the rest of them do.

Whether physical or mental, the leaving starts there. And it started there with Travis. He knew it did.

"Is something the matter?" she asked. "Nathan, if you need a new therapist—"

"I don't need therapy!" he spat. The other end of

the line went silent for a moment. "Sorry," he whispered.

"It's okay. I just...are you sure?"

"Very."

Tyler was not safe when he came over. That was the bottom line. The only line. He was not safe here. And so, he shouldn't ever be here. Landry had said he worried enough for two. Phoebe had said the same thing at Eliza's house. Maybe he'd been trying to *reason* for two people too.

"It doesn't have to be permanent," Hollie said.

"I know." This time, his voice barely choked out. "I know that. And I appreciate it. For right now though I think I just...I need some space."

"You can have that."

She was holding something back, Nathan knew, after all the years of dating then marriage then shared parenthood, he knew.

He didn't think it was his place to ask.

"Talk to you later," he just said.

A long silence lulled between them. Finally, Hollie said, "Yeah. Talk later."

He wasn't sure which one of them hung up the call after that. He set his phone on the counter and made his way back to the couch. From there he toppled down. His chest was tight, his head ached.

What did I just do? he thought as he buried his face in the couch cushions.

What the hell did I just do?

NOVEMBER

9

"They offered me a raise today."

Nathan looked up from his laptop at Travis, who wore a big, cheesy grin and a mustard yellow beanie. He said if he took it off now that they were inside, his hair would be a mess. *I'm an all-day hat kinda girlie, you know?*

Sometimes Nathan didn't know what to think of the way Travis spoke. Generational differences, he figured out pretty quickly.

Today the two were at a coffee shop called Black House Brews in Royal Oak, Michigan. It was Saturday afternoon around 3:00. Travis had tickets to go see an exhibit at the Lighthouse ArtSpace downtown that night. His friend had helped curate the exhibit and invited Travis last week to the grand opening with him. Nathan had little interest in modern art, but he had plenty of interest in seeing Travis that day. Lately, it seemed the two of them were seeing less and less of one another. Any time he could pocket with him was a win, and since they both had work to get done, they had agreed on a cute little coffee shop in the suburbs. Nathan ordered a macchiato. Travis had a pumpkin spice latte. They sat across from one another with their laptops perched open and Travis joked that he felt like he was back in college again.

"What, like two months ago?"

Travis rolled his eyes. "I graduated last year."

"I know." Though sometimes admittedly he did forget. It was easy to forget the details of a person like Travis when the whole ensemble was just so magnetic. "Did you always go on study dates in college? Feels kinda counterproductive to, you know, date stuff."

"No, not dates."

A silence permeated the bubble around them. *Not dates,* thought Nathan. Travis was staring at his laptop again now, so Nathan did the same. It had been Nathan's idea to accompany Travis today. *I want to see you,* he'd thought when Travis told him about the art gallery that night. *How about I join you for some work at a coffee shop?*

Over text, Travis had seemed excited. Relieved even that he would get to see Nathan in a different space. The last time they hung out without the use of Nathan's bed as a pastime had been short-lived. Travis was probably thinking along the same lines as Nathan now. It would be nice to just spend time together and talk. Like their first date had been. *Not dates though,* he thought now. *So then—*

"Congrats on the raise, though," he said.

"Thanks. Yeah, they said I've been doing really well and since Monica left, I've taken on a lot of her work too. It's cool that they recognize that." Monica was Travis's coworker at the advertisement company he worked for. Back when he and Nathan had been talking almost every day, Monica had been at her wits end. "Oh she's ready," Travis told him once. "Any day now, she's gonna blow." When she eventually did, it was unceremonious and unexpected, but Travis stepped up and took on probably more than he should've in her absence. It reminded Nathan of when he had his first job out of college. Back then you were so eager to prove yourself that sometimes you'd do anything.

"Well, seriously that's awesome." He reached a hand across the table and settled it on Travis's. He gave it a squeeze. Travis's mouth went taut. Nathan noticed. "What's up?"

Travis shook his head. "Not here."

"Oh. Okay."

He went back to his laptop then, only flitting his eyes up occasionally to see what Travis was doing. He spent most of the day on his phone and some of it on the computer. It was almost 4:30 when they decided to call it quits and head out.

"I'll drive you home," said Nathan as they walked out.

"Oh no, that's alright. I just ordered the Uber. It'll only be like ten minutes."

He turned back to Travis. "Okay, what's up?"

"What?"

"Earlier. With the hand. Now this. Something's going on."

"I just...I don't know. I feel like getting the raise and all that sort of made me realize how much is still out there for me."

"Right."

"And...maybe I don't want to be tied down to one person for right now. That's all."

Nathan's mouth was dry now. "Were you tied down?"

"No, I guess, I mean I wasn't."

"Because we never made anything official. I never

asked if you were talking to other guys." *Because I never wanted to know.*

Nathan knew how dating in the modern age went. Until there was a hard and fast label, there was a large margin for error. He learned that very quickly after his divorce. He wasn't going to jump right into another long-term, forever-type relationship. Now, though, his curiosity piqued. "Did you talk to other guys?"

"I don't need to answer that," said Travis.

"No, you don't." He was taken aback by Travis's aggressive tone. "I was just curious." Then, when Travis didn't say anymore, Nathan said, "So then you don't wanna see each other anymore?"

"I—" Travis's mouth opened and shut about three times before he settled on what to say. "I guess not."

"You guess?"

"Well I mean, you never know down the road. Like, I mean...I like you. I just. I don't know, I don't want this right now."

Why did it sound so similar to how he'd felt about Hollie towards the end?

There was an autumn chill in the air that bit Nathan's body. He had on a thin windbreaker, but underneath he wore a T-shirt and his arms were starting to freeze. Travis didn't look affected. Nathan sighed. "Okay. I appreciate you telling me that."

"I'm sorry."

"It's alright. Can I...can I hug you and say goodbye then?"

"Sure!" He sounded way too jovial.

They hugged. In that hug, Nathan felt nothing. A somber numbness was settling over his body. He couldn't help himself—in his mind he thought *there goes another one.*

He wasn't sure if Travis watched him walk away

after that—he imagined there was no way he *couldn't* at least glance—but he felt him on him the entire drive home. The feeling was so intense he went to take a shower as soon as he locked the front door. Showers used to be solace. They used to be something to look forward to.

Today, he shut off the water only a few minutes in and stood there, dripping, as the cool air tickled against his wet skin. He got out and wrapped a towel around himself and slumped against the counter. He didn't look at his reflection.

He wasn't sure he could.

———

Nathan was watching Survivor when there was a knock at the door.

He was in the middle of a marathon rewatch of one of his and Hollie's favorite seasons. There was a bowl of popcorn next to him on the couch, and his phone was charging upstairs. It had almost died during the lengthy Grindr binge he'd been on earlier in the night. It hadn't resulted in much—other than him getting off and leaving a lot of probably angry people on read after that—and it hadn't felt that great. Grindr never felt that great; even when you thought you met someone through it with a little extra sparkle in their eye, it was just a way to pass the time, really.

He got up reluctantly and went to the front door. He checked the peephole first and then swung the door open. Eliza was on the front porch. "Hi," he said. "Uh...what's up?"

"I haven't seen you in a while. Thought I'd stop by." She lifted a bottle of red wine in her left hand and smiled. "Can I come in?"

He stepped aside and then closed the door behind her.

"You haven't been back to D&D nights." They were in the kitchen now and he was getting two glasses down from the top shelf. Eliza twisted the top off the wine bottle. "We scare ya off that easy?"

"No," he said, "Just busy."

He set the glasses down in front of her and she poured. He noticed she was in what looked like silk pajama bottoms and a very thin T-shirt. "Dressed up for your visit, I see."

"Yeah," she said, lifted her glass of wine, and drank. "It was cold as fuck out there. So, uh, thanks for letting me in."

He nodded and took his own glass to the couch. He wasn't sure why Eliza was here tonight, but he figured he could use the company. She sat down across from him on the couch, and he noticed the wine level in her glass was already substantially lower. She gestured at the TV. "That's a good season."

"Yeah, my ex-wife and I used to watch it a lot."

Eliza sipped again. "You never talk about her."

"What? Hollie?"

"Aha! She has a name!"

He swirled his wine glass. "Uh huh. I guess, I mean there really isn't much to say."

"How long were you together?"

"I guess like eight years in total."

"And there's *nothing* to say...in eight years...?"

He sank further into the couch and hiked his feet up on the couch. He felt like a cinnamon roll sitting curled up like that. "That's the thing. There's plenty. But it's all sort of, I guess tainted."

"Hmm." Eliza sipped and the room went silent.

Something prodded at Nathan's mind. "Listen—about the other night."

"Don't mention it," she said.

"Well, no I...I mean I want to say I'm sorry for all that. There was a lot going on and I think I just sort of let it get to me. I hate that you had to see it."

She stared at him and nodded. Nathan didn't know Eliza that well. The few times they'd interacted were either at neighborhood things or in the middle of the night, when clearly no one was at their best. He glanced toward the stairs, and she followed his gaze. What did she think of that night? Had she seen it for what it was: a psychotic break? Or something else? God, what else could she see it as?

"You know," she said, "I'm always here to talk if you need that. We both work from home. We could have lunch some time or whatever."

Nathan realized he didn't even know what Eliza did for work. He figured now would be a good time to ask that, but his mind was preoccupied elsewhere. When he opened his mouth and words came out, they were, "I don't really think you'd understand. Sorry."

At first, he thought he was talking about the Lop-Sided man and the closet, but in his mind he saw Travis's face start to form. Travis had felt in so many ways like his one chance. He had been the type of normal life he could expect after Hollie. Meet a guy and connect on a physical level in ways he and Hollie had only ever done in sparse, fleeting moments, and then, only once things started to feel like they had a chance at sparking into something real...walk away. Travis had given him a taste of what was to come, and he'd eaten it up like a brand new dish at a Michelin star restaurant where the main ingredient was dairy and sure to wreck through his system in a matter of hours. You don't think about the aftermath while eating; you're too busy devouring. He shook his head.

"Try me," said Eliza.

Against all odds he smiled. "I just...that guy I was seeing called it off today. But it wasn't a breakup, so I don't need anything. It just feels..."

"Bad?"

"*Weird*. Nobody's called it off with me since Hollie." *And who really called it off then?* "Which is fine. He was too young. And he was right to do it."

"Doesn't make it any easier. Here." She stood and plucked his now empty wine glass from his hand. How did that happen? He didn't remember drinking the rest of it. As she swept into the kitchen and refilled the glasses she said, "It never gets easier, does it?"

"Well..." He took his glass when she handed it back. "Thanks. I think it does actually. I don't feel the way I felt when Hollie and I called it off. I guess I sort of feel like..."

Like what? Like he was experiencing all of this from behind the wrong set of eyes? Like all of a sudden, at twenty-nine the world had opened up and nobody was there to help him see how to navigate it? "It's hard to come out at twenty-nine," he said.

Eliza sat back. "I bet."

"No like...really hard. I lived a whole life one way, and it never felt perfect, but this doesn't either now. You hear about gay people from the 80s and 90s who were forced to be closeted well into their forties. That probably sucked, but it was a shared experience. Now, with some kids coming out as early as, fuck, I don't know...fourteen? Fifteen?"

"Some even younger," said Eliza.

"Great. I guess, I mean, they just have their own language at that point, and I just don't understand it."

Travis never asked what coming out was like for him. He just assumed he was entirely out. *Please*. His parents didn't know. Unless Hollie told them, which didn't seem like something she'd do, they probably never would. They weren't bad people, but they were *of a time*. Simple as that. How many questions had Landry asked him about his sexuality? He could probably count them on one hand. It was always about how difficult divorce was, how trying split households were on a kid's psyche. This. That. *Nathan, we need to get you some real help raising Tyler. That much is clear.*

Well—that much was already happening. He didn't need help with Tyler. He had never needed help with Tyler. Tyler was the one person he dealt well with since day one. He'd been the one who lulled him to sleep with a story each night; Hollie had been so jealous of that back in the day. "*I don't do anything special,*" he'd told her. "*Doesn't matter,*" she said back. *There had been jealousy leaking off her tone.* Tyler wasn't the problem; he never was.

"I don't know what I'm supposed to do. Or say. How I'm meant to act, you know? It's all confusing," he told Eliza.

"I think you just act like yourself still. Nothing has to change."

He groaned into the wine glass and took another sip. The red, leggy liquid stuck to the glass for a few moments after each sip before settling back at the base of the glass. *That's just not true,* he thought. He couldn't act like himself on Grindr. He couldn't go out with Travis and act like he always did. There was an expectation of freedom, of liberation, and maybe he just wasn't ready for it. Travis had been so free with his words, with his...his being. It was in the way he moved his hips and the way he held his face. There was a dance behind his eyes that Nathan didn't know the steps to. *What am I supposed to say now? Do you want me to do what you're asking or just make a joke about it?* Fuck, it was too much sometimes.

"That's not true," he said. "I just don't know."

Eliza's second glass was already done. She didn't get up to refill it again. Nathan figured they were almost out of wine now. He finished his glass too and they set both on the ottoman tray. When Eliza sat back on the couch, she curled up the way he was.

"You're figuring it out," she said. "That's okay."

Her eyes were suddenly far away.

"What's up?" he asked.

She opened her mouth, then closed it, then opened it again and said, "Do you regret leaving Hollie?"

"What? No, not at all."

"Really?"

He shook his head. "It wasn't working anymore." He left out the part where she technically left him and he hadn't wanted to file for divorce. Even after outing himself, he'd still wanted to stick it out. "I think maybe it was hard for me to realize that at the time," he said, "But once something isn't working it's pretty hard to get it back on track."

"But not impossible?"

"I mean...it probably was in our case."

Eliza gave a little half smile. "Right but like, not in every case."

"No, probably not. I don't know. I'm only *in* my case."

"Right, right." The faraway look returned to her eyes. Nathan wanted to ask what was wrong, but somehow, he felt unqualified, and so, they sat in sustained silence for three...four minutes—hell, maybe even longer. The ticking clock on the mantel screamed as the seconds passed. Eliza shifted on the couch. "I think we finished the wine."

"I think so too."

Her mouth fidgeted. "When did you know?"

"What? That I was gay?"

"No um...when did you know you were off track?"

In that moment, Nathan saw why she had come over tonight. "What's Ethan doing tonight?"

Her cheeks flushed red. "I'm not sure. He does his own thing most nights."

"And you don't like that?"

"No, it's not that."

"But it's part of it?"

A long pause. Nathan's breath caught in his throat.

"Things aren't going well between us," she said.

Nathan never really *met* Ethan, not fully. The only time he spoke to him was when he answered the door for him that night he went over for wine. That was a few words, and then a quick pass-off. Eliza didn't mention him, aside from when she told him they weren't ready for a baby, or that he was traveling for work, or how she needed people to keep her company Sunday nights because she couldn't be involved with how her husband was spending his. Hollie never did that to him. Even as everything fell apart, they rummaged through the wreckage together.

Eliza was crying now. Her tears fell slowly, and her words didn't crackle or break as she said, "He said he wanted a break last week. I—I didn't know what that meant. Then he asked me on Monday if I was happy with him. I...I mean what are you supposed to say to that?"

"Are you?"

"No! Of course not! How can you be happy with

someone when you *know* they're not happy with you? Isn't it part of loving someone to let them go when they aren't their best with you?"

Nathan didn't know. Had Hollie done that with him?

"We haven't talked since. I said I...I needed time to think. But I don't know. I just...you're the only person I know who's done this."

"What? Get divorced?"

She fell forward into one of his pillows. Her sobs echoed through the quiet house and Nathan shimmied closer and placed a hand across her back. He felt her spine quiver with each shaky breath. "It's okay," he said. "It's okay." *It'll pass,* he thought, but he couldn't tell her that.

When did it pass, he thought. *When did it really end?*

They talked for another hour once Eliza caught her breath. It turned out Nathan had more to say than he thought. He told her what the process would be like if they decided to go for it. He told her how long it took for him to feel like that part of his life was finally over. *"Sometimes it still doesn't though,"* he told her. *Like when he saw Hollie each time she dropped Tyler off, and for a moment she'd look at him with the familiar glint in her eye as before. The light might catch her hair and maybe a breeze would whistle by and perhaps she'd look more beautiful and younger than she had in years. It would take him back not to their marriage, but to when they first met. When he was her friend and slowly falling for her. It never felt wrong to fall for Hollie Smart. Little moments reminded him of that.*

"How long until you knew?"

Years, he almost said. *It took me years to know for sure.* But he knew that wasn't true even as he thought it. "I never really did," he said. "You don't know when a thing is wrong. It's just something in your bones. Sort of like if you always had an ache in your shoulder. You've lived with it for forever. Eventually it sort of fades from view, right?"

"Right."

"Until one day you suddenly realize...hey, my shoulder hurts. What the fuck's up with that? You ask around and people tell you their shoulders don't hurt like that. They have no idea what you're talking about. So, you see it for what it is. You're hurt. And you don't have to be."

"There's finally something to treat," she said.

He nodded as she burst into tears again.

Nathan's eyes had started to droop by the time he offered for her to spend the night. They were still on his couch, closer now though, and neither of them had said anything for a long time. The night had taken on a lethargic feel, sort of like a bubble had stretched around them and kept them hidden away from the rest of the world. In their bubble, time passed differently. He didn't dare glance at a clock; he knew it was too late to still be up. "You can sleep here tonight," he offered.

"Oh no, you don't have to do that," she said.

"You don't want to go back there, though," he said. And he was right; she didn't. "So," he breathed, "You can stay here. On one condition." She looked up at him then. "Call him. Tell him you're here. Don't make him worry about you all night."

"Oh he won't even—"

"No." Somehow, his mind landed on Tyler. When was the last time he'd spoken to his son? Why did he think his daddy never called anymore? "He will," he told Eliza.

She didn't question him further. "Okay," she said. "I'll call him."

As she did, he fluffed a few pillows and got a spare blanket from the closet under the stairwell. "Thank you," she said when he handed it to her. He nodded and offered her a curt smile. He was still thinking about Tyler.

"Thank you for calling him. It was the right thing to do."

She nodded back. "I should let you sleep now."

He showed her where the light switches were. "Turn 'em off whenever," he said. "There's glasses in the first cupboard above the dishwasher and a Brita in the fridge. Help yourself if you get thirsty." If she was Tyler he would fill a glass for her, leave it next to where she was sleeping, and worry about whether it would spill on her all night long. It only happened to Tyler once, back in his old apartment, but the way he woke up crying had sent Nathan into a spiral. *I should call him,* he thought. Then he glanced at the clock. *Tomorrow,* he added.

"Thank you," said Eliza.

He nodded. "Anytime." Then he rounded the couch and left her to head upstairs. As he climbed, he thought about what to say to Tyler when he did call. It hadn't been that long. A few weeks, three max? What was three weeks to a five-year-old? How did you make that time up? *Figure it out tomorrow. All for tomorrow.*

By the time he reached the top landing, the lights below were off.

The next morning, Eliza was sitting up on the couch by the time he came downstairs. He was dressed for work, hair still wet from the shower, and had almost forgotten about last night entirely, had it not been for the subtle ache in the back of his head from the cheap wine.

Something to treat, he thought.

"Hey," he said when he saw her. "Morning."

"Good morning." She yawned and the blanket he'd given her fell off her shoulders and around her waist.

"How'd you sleep?"

"Fine," she said. "I...it took a while to fall asleep."

"I bet." He passed her and went into the kitchen. There he opened the freezer and pulled out a bag of frozen berries. "Smoothie?"

"No that's alright. I need to head back."

"You sure? I promise they're good."

She was sure, though, and pretty soon she was standing up and using the bathroom. He heard the water run and when she came back out, her hair was damp and smoothed down. She had pulled it all to one side of her head and it dripped onto her left shoulder.

"Thank you. Again," she said. "I...I enjoyed talking last night."

He couldn't tell if she seemed more alert this morning or if her eyes were just like this in the morning. Something about them was different than they had been the night before, though. He slid a smoothie cup across the island at her. "Here. You need something after last night."

Her eyes glistened as she sipped the drink. "Thanks."

He crossed the kitchen and dug into the first drawer next to where Eliza was standing. He rummaged for longer than he should've through the disaster scene of loose papers, old credit cards, and whatever else he'd shoved in here since moving in. He hadn't even been here that long. How had it filled up so quickly? He pulled out a silver key and passed it over. "Here, keep it," he said.

"What's this?"

"Spare key. In case you, uh...hear anymore night terrors over here."

She looked at the key a second longer before reaching her hand out and plucking it free from his fingers. As she did, she smiled. "I don't think the nightstand can take another beating," he said.

"I don't think it could take the first one."

He rolled his eyes and closed the drawer. "Either way. If you need a place to run to, you can come over here. Even if I'm not home. Just...just text first."

"In case someone else is already over?"

"Fat chance. Just text first."

"I will. Thank you, again."

"Don't mention it."

He went back to the blender and threw in another cup of berries and the second half of the banana. Eliza sipped her own smoothie and wandered over to the kitchen table. She sat in one of the chairs just as he booted up the blender and the whirring sound filled the space.

"What do you have going on today?" she asked.

"Work," he said. He poured the smoothie in another cup. "The usual stuff. And I'm gonna call Tyler today."

"When's he coming over again?" she asked.

He paused and took a sip of his smoothie. He forgot the honey to sweeten it, but otherwise this morning it was good. "I don't know," he told Eliza. "I guess we'll find out soon."

10

_____

I t turned out five-year-olds didn't need excuses for why their daddies didn't call—his didn't, at least. Nathan had barely gotten out a "sorry, couldn't call bud—" before Tyler broke into a story about one of the kids on the playground and this new game they introduced him to.

"An-and-and then Sonny, because she's 'it' needs to run around the tree five times with her eyes closed. If she opens them, she has to do it again. It's hard though, Daddy, because you can't see where you're going, and you *want* to open your eyes!"

"Sounds like a fun game," he told him when Tyler was done recounting how whoever Sonny was had found him at the top of the jungle gym. But he slid down and then jumped, cutting his palms on the wood chips below, but not too deep and they didn't even hurt that bad. All so he could avoid being tagged and forced to run blindly around the base of that giant tree on the school yard because now he would be 'it'.

"*Yeahitwasfun!*" he said the whole sentence in a single breath. Then he paused and said, "Mommy wants to talk to you, Daddy, okay? Call again soon, yeah?"

"I will, bud. I promise."

There was shuffling on the other end of the line as Hollie took the phone back. In that time, Nathan threw on a jacket and made his way to the front door. It was one of those abnormally pleasant fall days today, and with no meetings left on his calendar, Nathan decided some fresh air was called for. It'll keep me up, he thought. *Just to stay moving.*

"Hey," said Hollie as he locked the door behind him and headed down the drive.

"Hi," he said.

The sun felt good on his face. The air was crisp but not bitter. There were leaves to crunch as he walked, and something about the day felt like one of those new beginning moments. This could be his new beginning, couldn't it?

"How are you?"

He thought about the question a moment before responding. "I've been better," he said. "But I've also been worse."

"Thanks for calling today. I know it meant a lot to him."

Nathan nodded. "I've been meaning to for a bit now. It was just...hard I guess."

"I get it. I do."

He was rounding the bend passed Eliza's house when he said, "And um, Hollie, I've been thinking..."

Eliza left shortly after breakfast that morning without much fanfare. He'd watched her go from the window to make sure she made it home alright. If he wasn't mistaken, she'd paused at the front door and fiddled with her key for longer than she needed to. He imagined Ethan wouldn't be home now, but there would be a definite conversation once he was. It wasn't his business to think about it now, though, so he tried to shake it from his head. There was no such conversation happening now. Now, as he walked past her house, things looked deathly still. *We both work from home...* Was she in there now, watching from one of the windows and seeing him pass?

"...I want Tyler to visit again."

"Nathan, are you sure?"

"I am. I understand how it looks, and how it probably feels after last time but...I want to throw him a birthday party over here."

Tyler's birthday was a few days after Thanksgiving. This year, it fell on a Saturday, and Nathan had been thinking for months about what to do when Tyler came over that weekend. He thought now about the closet. He couldn't have him sleep in his own room, that was for damn sure. But if there were other boys there, and maybe they were all sleeping over.

"A sleep over," he told Hollie. "With some of the closest friends he's got. They could come here. I'll move the couch and spread out some blankets and pillows. It'll be fun."

Hollie's tone was sharp on the phone. "No. I don't think that's a good idea, Nathan."

"It wouldn't just be me there, Hollie. I've made some friends in the neighborhood. I'm sure they would help me with it."

"Would they sleep over too?"

"They could if I asked."

There was a long silence on Hollie's end. Nathan passed under a vibrant red tree that had miraculously clung to all its leaves, then a browning one with only a few spots of orange and yellow yet. "Please, Hollie."

"I—Nathan, I'm just not sure." She was thinking about the police cars, about the phone call from Dr. Landry, about the red mark on his neck the last time she dropped him off and where he might've gotten something like that when he was supposed to be watching Tyler. *But Christ, Hollie, I'm not a different person now, am I? Nothing has to change...*Eliza said. He clenched his free hand into a fist and shoved it in his pocket.

"I'll call Dr. Landry tonight," he said. "Schedule something with her for later this week."

Another pause. "Does she take appointments so late in advance?"

"She will this time."

"You don't know that."

"And I won't until I ask."

There was a long pause. "Nathan, I don't know."

"Let me talk it out with her. Then I'll call you. Would that help?"

"I—yes. It would."

And so, it was settled.

Nathan hung up and spent the rest of his walk in silence.

"Thank you for squeezing me in." He followed Rebecca Landry into the familiar office and sat down across from her. She had a humidifier going in the corner and a few new plants scattered around his chair. He brushed one of the leaves aside and nestled further into the cushioned seat. "I know it's last minute."

"Oh, it's no bother," she said. "I'm glad you called, Nathan. Tea?"

"Um, what kind?"

"Peppermint or oolong."

"I'll take peppermint. Thanks."

She poured two mugs and passed one off to him. He blew the top of it and tried to take a sip. The liquid scalded the tip of his tongue, and he drew back. He set the mug on the table next to him and smiled.

It was Thursday evening now. When he first called Landry after getting home from his walk on Monday, she hadn't picked up. Figured. It was too late in the day, and she had probably finally wrapped up her appointments and was eager for a relaxing drive and then an evening at home. He spent the night workshopping what he'd say when he got ahold of her the next day.

On Tuesday he made sure to call in the morning. *"I'd like to set up another meeting time now,"* he told her. *"And I'm sorry for storming out…"*

She hadn't seemed like she needed an apology, but there was a business-only tone to her voice over the phone that he didn't quite like. She carried that tone into their meeting now, and as she sat down with her tea in her lap, she folded one leg over the other and tilted her head to the side, as if silently examining him. The look ate at him until she turned to the side and set her mug down next to the same moleskin notebook from before. Her pen jutted out from the bottom, and she used it to flip the notebook open to the most recent page she'd left off on.

A drawing fell out.

One of Tyler's drawings. It fluttered down to the ground and Landry bent to pick it up. "You left this one here," she said, and handed it back.

"Thanks."

The drawing wasn't much different than the others. The closet door was still visible, so was the window on the side of Tyler's bedroom. There was no bed though. Instead, dark, spindly flames licked up from the spot on the floor where the bed should be. The closet door sat ajar, and a hand was poking out from behind it.

"You were right," Landry said, "There's something disturbing about that drawing."

"Kids," he said and set the drawing aside. "They're pretty imaginative."

He met Landry's stern gaze—dared her to say more. He wouldn't be the one to broach the topic further. He was here on a peacemaking mission. *I have to win my son back.*

"Mhm...so, do you wish to continue where we left off or...?"

"I wanna talk about the last few weeks."

And so, he did. Whether Dr. Landry asked or not, he told her about his breakup with Travis, which wasn't really a breakup, but he couldn't find a more appropriate label. Then he mentioned Eliza's visit on Sunday and his subsequent talk with Hollie and Tyler. He mentioned night terrors and waking up in places he didn't remember falling asleep. He did *not* mention the closet lock, or the Lop-Sided man, or the fact that his night terrors sometimes left him feeling more awake than real life did.

"I woke up on Monday sort of feeling...refreshed," he finished.

"That's good. Why do you think that is?"

"I think it worked its way through. And I think...I think I forgot how far I'd come."

As she jotted down the last thing he said, he noticed Landry smile. She flipped a few pages back in the notebook. "You know, Nathan, there are always going to be dark times."

He nodded.

"And I think what's most important is reminding

yourself that you aren't a monolith. You aren't the first person to experience what you're experiencing, and you can always find someone else who might be able to help."

He thought about what he'd told Eliza the other day about coming out later. It wasn't just that. He had come out with a kid attached to him. He carried the baggage of a past relationship, of a life that he couldn't live any longer. How long had he been walking around since then wondering if anyone had ever felt the same way? Almost like gay men with kids didn't exist, or nobody had been divorced once or twice in their lives. Did he look at them and think, oh that's different because they aren't me?

"How do you find those people?" he wondered aloud.

Rebecca Landry shook her head. "It doesn't say that part here."

"Huh?"

"Nathan, you said that earlier. On..." she paused, "March 6th."

"How do you..."

"Wrote it all down. You said that months ago."

She stood up and handed over the moleskin notebook he'd glared at for the last year now. Pages and pages of ridicule and false prescriptions...he thought.

"I like to write down the things people say, because someone told me years ago that we usually work our feelings out best on our own. Sometimes we just need a mouthpiece to deliver the help."

He took the notebook and flipped through the pages. Every page was dated and filled with quotations that apparently *he* had said.

. . .

FEB 16 *He's been drawing a lot lately, and he comes up to me sometimes and wants to "work" next to me so he'll make me get out my laptop and pretend to be at work; I don't know what he's drawing but he's doing something and smiling a lot, and that's enough for any parent, ya know?...*

APRIL 11 *I didn't have a good day today and I don't know why; sometimes I don't think people know why, their days are just bad. Maybe that's okay, right?...*

JUNE 3 *Hollie doesn't get it, that's why. I can't talk to her the way I used to and it sucks because I feel like I lost my best friend more than I lost my wife even...*

AUGUST 28 *Today was a good day. No, I don't know why yet. Maybe I'll figure it out by the time I lay down tonight.*

And on...and on...Nathan flipped until he closed the book, looked up at Landry who was now sat back on her chair with her legs re-crossed and her cup of steaming peppermint tea in her lap again. She took a sip from it, and he saw the smile painted across her eyes.

"You can keep that, you know," she said.

He almost let out a laugh. "I think I might."

"I give them out after a year or so. I would've the last time you were here but...well...did you ever figure out why that day wasn't so great?"

He stared at her. *No,* he thought. Then came the image of the Lop-Sided man, crawling out of unlocked closet and creeping toward Tyler's bed. He shook his head. "I didn't, no. But this made today pretty good." He shook the notebook like it was some gold medal and he was standing on the Olympic podium.

"I'm glad."

"But, uh, you don't need it to take more notes?"

Landry set her tea down again and reached behind her chair. She pulled a fresh moleskin still clad in plastic from the ground and waved it up in mimicry of him. This one was a burnt orange color.

"Please, I always keep a spare. So..." She unwrapped the notebook and threw the crinkled paper to the side. It missed the trash can she was aiming for by a few inches and fluttered down next to it. She would get that later. She cracked the notebook's spine and reached for her pen. "How have things been with your son?"

He called Hollie on the way home to talk. She didn't have much time, so he said he could make it quick. He recapped the therapy session and told her what Landry suggested about adding a new *medication* to his second year with her.

"How do you feel about that?" she asked.

"I don't know. Can only help, right?" Really, he'd cringed at the idea, but didn't see a way out necessarily. The longer he sat with the idea of talking to a doctor about getting on some sort of mood stabilizer, the stronger he felt it was the right decision.

"I can't say much. I'm not a doctor," said Landry, "But you wouldn't be the first person I've talked to that has seen more progress in their second year because of the addition of a medical professional."

"Right."

Then the two talked about logistics. He wanted to throw this party; Hollie would have to help make it happen. She wasn't sure, even as she threw out names of other boys she could ask, if it was the right thing to do. *She's still thinking about the police cars*, thought Nathan. She saw them rushing up, lights blazing, horns blaring. It wasn't like that, but it didn't matter that it wasn't. It didn't matter that Tyler slept through the whole thing. What if it happened again and there were other boys there this time? That wasn't just bad on Nathan's part anymore. Now it hurt Hollie too.

After all this time they were still a team.

"I don't know, Nathan."

"I know that. And I don't expect you to know. But... can you trust me still, Hollie?"

Seconds ticked by...minutes even, before finally she said, "I'll drop them off Saturday at seven."

Before heading home, Nathan pulled into an old shopping center where years ago, most of the shops went out of business. It was the kind of strip mall you couldn't find on the newly paved roads of any up-and-coming suburb. When he got out of the car, he took special care to make as little noise as possible when shutting his door. When the little bell chimed as he walked inside the only remaining shop in the center, he flinched. It took ten minutes for him to get in, get out, and sound that chiming alarm again.

Only when he was back in his car did he breathe easier; only then did he notice the shop windows were barred off like some sort of state prison tucked in the middle of nowhere. He set a plastic bag on the passenger seat, and as he whipped around in the parking lot, the contents spilled out. He reached down and tucked his brand new revolver back into the bag. Then, with his hand still holding the gun in place behind the plastic the whole way, he drove home.

11

"I love you too buddy...Hey, I gotta let you go now, but I'll see you in just a few days right? Right. I love you. Happy Thanksgiving."

Tyler handed the phone back to Hollie then. "Spencer and Adam's mom's agreed. They think it sounds fun."

"Thank God," he said. "So what? That makes five of them?"

"Four. Evan cancelled. His sister's got a piano recital that Sunday. They don't want to have to drive to pick him up first."

"Makes sense."

So, four boys were coming...that meant he would need to clear enough space for the four of them...He paced the living room while still on the phone, not saying anything, just measuring mentally.

Hollie cleared her throat and said, "Nathan, I do have to go."

He jolted. "Right, Thanksgiving. I get it."

"Are you doing something?"

"Not really. It's fine, Hollie. I like it that way, you know."

"I know."

She sounded sad when she said it. Hollie and Tyler were going to Hollie's parents' house the same as they always did. Nathan had sent his own parents a text message wishing them a *Happy Thanksgiving* but had not received an invite back. Maybe they weren't doing anything this year; maybe they just didn't want him present.

Probably assumed he wouldn't come.

"I'll talk to you later," he told Hollie. "Let me know if anything changes. Happy Thanksgiving."

"You too."

He hung up the phone then and kept mentally measuring the space. He didn't think about the fact that it was Thanksgiving and the rest of the country was feasting while surrounded by family and friends and loved ones for the rest of the day.

The party was just two days away.

He had preparations to make.

He bought balloons and streamers the next day. Party City wasn't open on Thanksgiving, but the roads were just as empty that Friday. He bought four bags of balloons in as many colors as he could find, six rolls of streamers—mostly in red and blue—and on his way out asked the clerk how much the helium balloons would run him.

"I'll be back for some of those," he said. Then he texted Eliza asking whether the helium balloons were even worth it.

Worth it, she sent back. *So, so, worth it.*

And so, he went back the next day. By then, his house was cleaned, then mussed up again by party extravagance. It looked like a circus clown threw up across the banister and the living room floor. There were enough balloons for you to kick with every step. The banister, the mantel, the kitchen table and chairs —all of it was concealed behind red and blue streamers.

He returned once to buy another two wheels once the six he'd originally left with ran out. That was right before Eliza and the others arrived. Penny had jumped first at the chance to come to a kid's party.

"I used to love throwing these when Charlie was little."

Charlie was her now twelve year old daughter who Nathan had never met, but felt like he'd know as soon as he did from all Penny talked about her. She had Penny's face and her husband's height. "Luckily she got these legs though," said Penny the last time Charlie was brought up. She stroked her own rather lengthy limbs as she said it and sent eye rolls spinning around the room. Nathan, for his part in the matter, couldn't help but laugh. Helen came too, though she was more there for the sake of decorating and getting wine drunk before the kids showed up.

"Any chance to get outta the house is good enough for me."

She came in last and set a gentle hand on Eliza's shoulder when she did. Then she hugged Nathan and Penny. When she walked away to put both her wine and the ice cream cake she'd picked up on her way over in the proper places, Nathan glanced at Eliza. Had she told somebody else about her and Ethan? There had been tenderness in that gesture that seemed to suggest it.

"Come on," Helen called from the kitchen. "I got wine. Before the kiddos get here!"

"They aren't due for another hour," said Nathan. He followed the others into the kitchen regardless.

Once the girls had their fill—Nathan drank nothing—they went back to work.

While they were hanging the last of the streamers in a fringe arch across the entrance from the foyer to the living room, Hollie texted that she and the boys were twenty minutes out.

"They're almost here!" he shouted.

Eliza gave a half-hearted holler and Penny clapped. Helen was too busy standing on a small step stool on her tippy toes with the last streamer in hand. Nathan took a deep breath and tried not to panic. He thought about the boys who were coming, about seeing Tyler again. Then, his mind traveled to the closet upstairs and the last errand he'd run the other day, the revolver he had stored in Tyler's bedside table.

It was almost time.

Nathan stood on his driveway as they rolled up. It felt a bit like a first date, when she drove up in her dad's borrowed car right on time, even though she'd been waiting for the last ten minutes around the block. You were just going down the road, probably to grab shakes and walk around the mall, but she'd wanted to pick you up. It gave her a slice of the power, and you were happy to oblige because you didn't want to drive in front of her and make an ass out of yourself, maybe get your hands too sweaty on the steering wheel that they left a greasy stain or weren't fit for holding later on in the night. At least, Nathan was always eager to let his dates pick him up. Maybe that's why he'd wanted to pick Travis up the other day. *That way it could be different.*

He felt those type of nerves now and arched his back as he waved at Hollie in the driver's seat. His spine crackled, probably from the cold. Should've grabbed a light jacket before waiting out here.

Hollie waved back, and he caught a "save me" expression from her even behind the hazy glass. He smiled. Four small boys in one car; he'd need saving too.

Tyler was the first one out.

"Daddy!"

He ran to him and collided with his pelvis. "Doh! Hey-ey buddy, how've you been?"

"Good Daddy!" Then, he looked up and caught a glimpse of the living room through the front door. Two balloons had bounced their way onto the front step. A few of the streamers billowed in the wind. "Whoa..."

"Happy birthday, Bud!"

Another boy ran up dressed in a red shirt, light jeans, and a Red Sox hat. "Hi," he said.

Nathan bent down to both boy's level. "Nice to meet you," he said. He held out a hand and the boy smacked it with a high-5.

"I'm Spencer."

"Nice to meet you, Spencer."

The other two boys ran up shortly after. Adam and Isaac. Nathan guessed Isaac was in the lead and Adam was the pudgy boy a few steps behind. He had no way of knowing, especially as all four boys marveled at the display in the front door and one of the two of them—pudgy Adam—said, "Whoa check it out!"

"Can we, Daddy?" asked Tyler.

"Of course."

As they ran off, Hollie walked up. Her car beeped twice as she locked it. She wore a grey cardigan and black jeans. "Hey," she said, "Sorry we're a bit late."

"All good. Party doesn't start till you're here. So, you're right on time."

She smiled weakly. "It looks great," she said.

"Come on in and see. You don't have to leave right away."

"No that's okay. This is your day with him. I want it to be special." In a lowered voice so that no one could hear she added, "You're doing alright?"

The flash of a gun lit through his mind. "Better than ever," he said.

He wasn't sure she believed him, but she didn't put up a fight. "Good, I'm glad."

"Hey." Eliza poked her head through the doorway. "Sorry to bother but—"

"—No worries—"

"Oh, hi, you must be Hollie?" Eliza stepped out and offered her hand. Hollie took it and smiled. "I'm Eliza. I live next door."

"Oh, fun," said Hollie. "I was just heading out."

"What? No, you should stay for a bit."

"I really shouldn't." Nathan saw the strain in Hollie's face. Of course, she wanted to stay. It was Tyler's birthday and his birthday party. What kind of mother wanted to leave him for a thing like that? She glanced at him though and his mouth tightened.

"I understand," he said.

Eliza did not. Her body appeared around the door frame as she leaned against it, arms crossed and a friendly smile across her face. Her eyes darted between Nathan and Hollie. "Come on, just until the pizza's here."

"I thought you said the pizza was already here?"

"On its way. I said it was in the oven."

"Oh." They'd ordered Dominos at peak rush hour on the Saturday night after Thanksgiving, when nobody in America felt much like cooking; a delay made sense.

"Really I should head home," said Hollie. "I've got a few things I need to get done and—"

"Mommy!" Tyler rushed past Eliza and nearly knocked her off the doorstep.

Nathan sidestepped his son as he rushed into his mother's hip with all the force of a now six-year-old hurricane. *Six*, thought Nathan. When in the world did that happen? A balloon on a ribbon trailed him and bounced leisurely off Hollie's face. She batted it away and started smiling.

"Mommy, will you draw hopscotch for us?"

Nathan noticed the chalk in his son's other hand. The purple dye smeared across his fingers.

Nathan stepped forward. "I got a fresh set for the boys." Then, down to Tyler he said, "How did you already break into that?"

Tyler offered him a naughty glance and giggled as he head butted into Hollie's stomach.

"I'm sure Daddy can draw one for you," Hollie said.

"Not like you..."

Hollie looked up and Nathan met her eyes. There was pleading behind them, and he nodded in silent response. Since the divorce, they kept their lives separate. When Tyler was with him, he wasn't with Hollie and vice versa. His calls to talk to him on the weeks he didn't visit were the only times their two worlds collided. But never here. Never when it was Nathan's turn.

"Alright," Hollie said. "Is the chalk out back?"

Nathan nodded. "Better be. There's a little concrete patch in the yard. Are the tables all set up there?" he asked Eliza, who nodded vigorously and then turned toward the house.

"Here, I'll show you," she said.

And Hollie followed. She held Tyler's hand as she walked inside, and a moment later Nathan followed. The same bubbling up of anxious first-date nerves simmered inside him, but he shut the door and followed his ex-wife and his son to the backyard.

A half hour later and Hollie was still there. Now, the sun dipped dangerously low on the horizon, but the chill in the autumn air seemed only to touch the adults as they crowded around the foldable table they'd decked out with party streamers and star-shaped confetti and watched the four boys chase each other around the yard. Eliza walked back to the porch and heaved out a heavy breath.

"Can't keep up?" joked Nathan. She shot him a narrow look.

"At least I ran with them."

"I won two games of hopscotch," he said.

"I think they let you win," said Penny from the other side of the table. She sat in one of the folding chairs and sipped at something in one of their plastic cups. Earlier he'd watched her pop open another bottle of wine and offer some to Hollie. She'd declined, but now sat next to Penny with her arms tucked tight against her chest and a slight chatter to her teeth. She hadn't gotten up to go yet, and Nathan found the longer she was there the happier he became.

Sometimes Tyler would run to her and give her a hug just because. Others, he'd bang into Nathan and try and drag him out onto the lawn.

"No no," he told him for probably the twelfth time. *"You guys are too fast for me. I can't keep up."*

Then he'd run off with the others and pick up whatever game they'd invented like he hadn't missed anything at all. It felt almost...nice, normal even, to have Hollie there. And though the two hadn't spoken since they got to the backyard, just having her there was enough.

Maybe we can still do this after all.

"Pizza's almost here," said Eliza. She pocketed her phone and said, "I'm getting a drink. Anyone want one?"

"I'll have one," Nathan said. When everyone else shook their heads—except for Penny who shook her still sloshing cup instead—he followed Eliza inside and into the kitchen.

"I like her," said Eliza. She grabbed a two-liter bottle of Pepsi from the fridge. The kids weren't allowed to have caffeine, so any of the caffeinated sodas Helen and Penny had brought over had to be kept inside. "Hollie, I mean."

"Yeah," said Nathan. "I'm glad."

"How's it for you? She doesn't come over much, does she?"

He shook his head. "I mean...never. Think this is the first time she's seen this side of the house since I moved here. Maybe once to make sure it was kid proofed and all, but other than that..." He trailed off and looked through the window over the sink that overlooked the backyard. Hollie was talking to Helen now and one of the boys ran up. He couldn't make out what they were saying from here.

"Well, maybe she can come over more often." Eliza passed him a cup of dark soda. "Figured you didn't want ice."

"Thanks," he said.

As he spoke, the same boy from before raced through the back door and blew past the kitchen.

"Hey!" Nathan called. "What's up?"

He stepped into the hall just as Tyler ran up behind him, following his friend around the bend and up the stairs. As he did, he shouted, "They're in my closet! It's right upstairs and—"

And then Nathan stopped hearing what his son was saying. *Closet.* He set his cup down and ran down the hall like a sprinter after the gunshot fired. *Closet.* So far, he'd kept Tyler away from any thoughts of his bedroom upstairs. The boys were sleeping in the living room, on the couch or the floor with sleeping bags and comforters galore. There was no need to go up there. Nobody would be going up at all.

"Tyler!" he shouted. "Wait!"

He was at the bottom of the stairs when he heard a door slam shut upstairs.

No.

"Nathan?" came Eliza's voice behind him. "What's wrong?"

He ignored her, took the steps two at a time, and was almost at Tyler's door when it started to open again. Tyler and the other boy—Adam, he thought— were walking out with a plastic frisbee and a jump rope in their hands. They were startled when they saw Nathan.

"Daddy!"

"Whatcha got there, bud?" His breath came out ragged, and an ache started low in the corner of his head. He saw light streaming out of the bedroom.

"Ms. Helen knows how to jump rope real good," said Adam. "She's gonna show us."

"Yeah, and I forgot I had this!" Tyler held up the frisbee and smiled.

He's smiling, thought Nathan. Everything was fine. "Alright," he breathed. "Just...be careful with it, okay? And if it goes over the neighbor's fence, you have to ask them to go get it."

Tyler nodded vigorously and hugged Nathan on his way past him. He and Adam bolted down the stairs and past Eliza as she looked up at Nathan.

"All good?" she asked. Another figure walked up beside her. Hollie's face was melancholy as she stood next to Eliza, her expression puzzled.

"Yeah," he breathed out. "All good." Then, he looked at Hollie and said, "Heading out?"

She nodded. "Can we talk first?"

A different kind of dread filled him then. He reached into Tyler's bedroom and shut off the light. He noticed the closet was already closed again. Had the boys done that before racing out?

"Sure," he said. "Let me walk you out."

There were certain silences that felt louder than others. The one that followed them out to Hollie's car was vast, and seemed to echo with a weight Nathan's shoulders couldn't carry.

Hollie was the one who broke it.

"They're nice," she said. "I like them for you."

"Yeah," he said, though he wasn't sure what she was implying by that. *You don't have to like them for me anymore. I can choose them on my own.* "Thank Eliza for introducing me, I guess."

"She's good for that. Is she...?"

"My neighbor." They reached her car. Hollie turned back to face him. "And my friend."

Her face was somber with understanding, and he was reminded again why she didn't have a part in the life he was building for himself. *Would it be better, my dear, if I was sleeping with her? Would it at least make it okay if I still liked to sleep with women?*

Only you—he thought. *It was always you. Until it wasn't.*

The same silence stretched between them again. Nathan was reminded of those first few months together. He didn't have a car in college, so he'd walk Hollie to hers. After each date she'd drop him off, he'd linger, and they'd kiss against the car door. He smiled from the memory. Hollie didn't ask why. He suspected maybe she was remembering the same thing.

Then she broke the silence again.

"Nathan, I have to tell you something."

"Hmm?"

"I'm being transferred for work."

"You—already? Didn't they say that doesn't come till like...years in?"

"It is years now. I passed my two-year last month."

"Oh, damn. Well, congrats."

"Thanks."

"Where are they moving you to?"

She looked down. "Austin."

"I—in...Texas?"

She nodded.

"That's...wow. I thought they were mostly local."

"They're expanding into other markets, and right now if you wanna go into tech you're goin' to Austin. Medical sales are huge there."

Nathan's head spun. "Well...seriously, congrats. You can get away from Detroit winters."

"They aren't so bad."

He laughed. "No, I mean I always liked them. Except that one. Remember the vortex."

"It was not the vortex. You always say this."

"When they shut classes down and you stayed at my place for like three days? I'm pretty sure that was the polar vortex."

"No, that was years after!" She was smiling now, and something about that smile still pulled at his heartstrings all these years later. "It was just a really really cold couple of days."

"Like negative 40, right?"

"Something like that. I know your roommate did the boiling water trick. Turned it into snow. Almost got frostbite in the process."

"Yeah...Garrett wasn't the smartest there."

She looked down again and then glanced back at the house. Nathan kept looking right at her. "Tyler...?"

"He's coming with me," she finished. "The company is giving me till August to move down there. So, it'll be after the school year's done."

It was like a gun was pressed to his chest, the way his stomach plummeted. He glanced back at the house, and as he did, he heard a child scream with laughter and then the shuffle of many feet chasing after it.

"What about his friends?" he asked, because really he didn't have it in him to ask what he was actually thinking.

What about me?

"He's young. He'll make new friends."

"Right..."

"I'm really sorry to drop this on you now. I thought

it would be better to tell you now than a few months down the road. It's still fresh for me too. It's taking some adjusting to, I don't know, get used to."

"Right."

If she kept talking then, he didn't hear her. His vision went narrow, and his heart felt just about ready to give out. "When will I get to see him then?"

She opened her mouth, but nothing came out. Another high pitched laugh echoed out the door and down the drive. She looked in the direction of the house, then down, and shook her head. "Nathan, we can figure that out later."

"Seems like the kind of thing we should figure out now."

She met his eyes.

"What if I don't want my son being taken away from me."

"He's not being taken away from you."

"Great, so when will I get to see him? Just holidays? Random days you visit your parents?"

"Nathan, please..."

"I'm just saying...It feels an awful lot like this decision didn't really involve me and now I just have to deal with it."

"Of course it didn't involve you! This is my life. *Mine*. Your life is here. You're building a new one. You have friends now. You clearly had some fun the last few months—" she absentmindedly lifted a hand to her neck, "—you've got a great house. You have freedom. Besides, God, you didn't even see him for the last month anyways."

"That wasn't my decision."

"No, it wasn't."

"You decided that."

But she shook her head again. "No. Tyler did."

"What?"

"He told me he didn't like coming over and he was scared to keep doing it."

Scared. He was scared. "Not of me," he said.

"Then what of?"

He bowed his head. "That's bullshit," he said. Tyler? Tyler was the one who didn't want to come over anymore? Tyler, who was probably excited now to move to Texas and see some place new. Tyler, who wasn't going to miss his daddy the way his daddy was going to miss him.

"It's okay," said Hollie. "You're allowed to have other priorities now. I get it."

"What?" He lifted his head. "What other priorities do I have? Living a life with the fucking scraps you left me of yours?"

He knew his voice was rising now, and he tried to think about anything else. He couldn't though. All he saw was Hollie picking Tyler up when the weekend was done and whisking him away forever. *Play your cards right or you might not see him after today. Play 'em right or you'll be on your own...for real this time.* But how did you play your cards right when you weren't dealt any cards to handle?

"You kicked me out of your home. You let me see our son—*ours*—for four, sometimes five fucking days a month. You don't answer my calls. You take ages for a text. And then you come here and tell me it looks like everything I have is going well? Well? The other day you refused to let me see my son because you thought I was falling apart. What changed between then and now? Huh? Is it how clean my fucking neck is? No hickeys this time, huh? That all it takes with you?"

"No."

"Because it feels like that! You're so mad at me for just being myself that—"

"I am not! I don't care that you're gay. I want you to be happy. God-dammit, Nathan. Excuse me for feeling weird that my ex-husband is seeing someone else."

"I'm not seeing anyone!"

"Great. I'm sorry to hear that. And I'm sorry for being uncomfortable. This is why this isn't working. It hasn't been working. I can't keep coming over here and calling and texting and acting like everything is normal when it isn't. You haven't asked one thing about my life in months."

"Bullshit."

"It's not."

It wasn't. Nathan ran through his routine calls now. He asked how she was in the vaguest terms possible, then she passed the phone off to Tyler, or he started talking about Tyler, or asking when he got to see him again. He didn't know how well she was doing at work; he wasn't sure if she was going on dates or making new friends or anything. With her he kept it strictly business.

He shook his head. His eyes were shut now, but he still saw the silhouette of Hollie emblazoned against them. "I'm sorry for that. I think it was just...too painful to ask."

"I know."

"But that doesn't mean I wasn't curious. I mean, fuck, Hollie, I wanted to make things work with us. I would've stayed in the house. I would've stayed to-gether. I wanted to—"

"You didn't love me anymore."

The space deadened between them. For a brief moment, Nathan was no longer in his driveway, but in another house, in the bedroom, with his wife standing before him with her head down, her fists shaking, and their baby son crying in the other room. He registered Hollie was crying, and the urge to wrap her in a hug bit hard at his stomach. He fought against it though. She would hate him for that. She probably already did.

"That's not true, Hollie."

"It is."

"I still love you."

She shook her head. "But not the way I loved you. Nathan, you stopped doing that a long time ago."

Feet pitter-pattered against the concrete. He looked up and he and Hollie turned to the front door. Tyler was running back inside. Nathan heard him sniffle, almost like he was starting to cry.

"Was he standing there?"

Hollie didn't answer. "Tyler! Wait!" She ran after him. A moment later, Nathan followed.

When Nathan hit the foyer, Hollie was already heading up the stairs. There was the loud thud of a slamming door.

A bedroom door.

No.

"I've got it," said Hollie.

Nathan nodded but wanted to tell her to *get it* somewhere else, anywhere else. Get Tyler out of that room; he shouldn't be there.

Then his ex-wife vanished down the hall and he heard a knocking on the door. It must've swung open, because a second later, he heard the soft click of it once again shutting into place.

12

_____

When he was eleven, Nathan went to a Red Wings game with his dad. He got the tickets through work and told him the morning of. "Gear up after school, kiddo, we're gonna watch some hockey!"

It was all he thought about the rest of the day.

When they got to the stadium though, a pit formed in the middle of Nathan's stomach. "I don't wanna go," he told his dad through almost queasy breaths. They had just paid for parking in a dusty lot with only a few cars and a twenty dollar cover charge. Nathan was in the backseat doing his best not to fall apart. He noticed the crowds moving on the pavement toward the stadium. His dad ignored him and got out of the car. Nathan had no choice but to follow.

As they walked to the stadium, he tugged at his dad's bomber jacket. "I don't wanna," he said, to still no response.

Instead, his dad turned around and told him about what real hockey games were like. "_They're not like they are on TV. You won't see everything that's happening unless you really pay attention. But when something does happen, man you'll feel it deep in your gut. It's like a rollercoaster. You remember Cedar Point last summer, right?_"

Nathan had just grown tall enough to ride most of the coasters last summer; he'd walked away weak-kneed and sick to his stomach, but with a flush in his cheeks and a vigor in his eyes that kept him up well past his bedtime that night. Now, he had the same sick-to-his-stomach feeling, but the vigor was gone. Behind him, someone started chanting words he couldn't make out. Soon, more voices joined in. He clung to his father's arm as they lined up with the rest of the intense hockey fans. He looked back at the chanting men and saw two of them in the middle of a gathering crowd. They wore rubber masks with horns and spikes coming out of their animalistic nostrils. One of them turned to him and Nathan swore when it huffed out a breath, smoke spilled out from under the mask. He turned back to his dad and gave his arm a tug.

"Nathan, it's fine."

"But Dad—" he turned back to the monster men. A police officer was asking them to remove the masks while in line. The first one peeled off the rubber skin and his face underneath was deep burgundy, white lines creased across where the rubber had sat. The other tugged his mask up on top of his head. He still looked like he had two faces as he joined the line.

They had just made it to the main doors when Nathan's dad said, "Gonna be a good one tonight."

He was talking to the broad-shouldered black woman scanning their tickets. She was wearing a security uniform and had her short hair styled in wispy feather-like curls. She raised both her eyebrows and smiled. Then she looked down at Nathan.

"You excited for tonight?"

He nodded because he didn't know what other option he had. Then he jumped when his dad clapped him on the back.

"Nate's been gearing up all week! Haven't ya?"

"Um, uh huh."

The woman ushered them in without another word. "Tickets!" she shouted as soon as they were through. Nathan kept his head down and gripped his dad's arm tighter.

His dad looked up as they moved through the crowded stadium. There were numbers hanging in the alcoves. "We're looking for 121," he told Nathan. Little Nathan did his best to look up also, but when he did his footsteps slowed down too much to maintain pace with his father, and he ended up stumbling forward and almost onto the ground. As he did, a woman with dirty blonde hair and a shirt that was cut low in the middle and revealed the fleshy line of fat in the middle of her chest, almost tripped into him. She was holding a tray of chips and nacho cheese, and if she hadn't reacted in the last moment, the warmed cheese would've been dripping onto Nathan's head right about now. The whole thing made him want to cry.

"Here we are."

Nathan turned with his father, and they descended a steep staircase. As they did, the stadium opened up. Bleachers circled the ice rink, and he could see some of the team members practicing on either end. One of them overcorrected his shot as he started to spin out and ended up flat on his ass. A few crowd-goers cooed when they saw it. Nathan felt his whole body flinch.

"Is he okay?" he asked.

"Huh? Oh yeah, they're fine. It's all padding under their uniforms."

Nathan wasn't too sure. The player took a few too many seconds to get back up to be perfectly okay.

When they found their seats, Nathan plopped down and vowed not to move the rest of the night. His dad turned to him and said, "I'ma go find us some food. What do you want? Hot dog?"

"I don't like hot dogs."

"Oh, come on, it's the thing here."

I wanna go home, thought Nathan. There were so many people around. Behind him, there was a couple shouting at the rink even though nothing was happening. He let out an unsteady breath. "Okay."

He watched his dad's bobbing head melt into the stadium crowd.

At first, everything felt fine. Nathan sat there, looked around, and told himself he would be back soon. He was in his seat. All he had to do was stay here and it would be just fine. Then, he spotted a man in one of those rubber masks coming toward him in the aisle. His heart started racing and his vision blurred for just a second. The man's body was normal, barrel shaped and wide, but human just the same. His face was concealed by a rubber bull mask. It had the same horns as the ones before, but instead of a ring in the nostril and spikes in the eyebrow bones, it protruded out further into a real enough looking snout. The mask was a deep brown color with tawny highlights. Nathan saw the bull's eyes move from underneath.

He sat back in his chair and stood his ground.

Then the masked man spoke. "Aye, I think you're in the wrong seat."

What little strength was left in Nathan plummeted. "Um..."

He looked up the stairs. His dad must've been heading back, right? Right?

"You in 118 maybe?"

Then he looked back at the bull. The mask jiggled

as the man looked down at him, like the kind of fleshy protrusion you'd find in a freak show not on Animal Planet. When the man breathed, the whole thing pulsated with sentient life.

"Hey, kid can you hear me?"

When Nathan didn't respond the man reached a hand up to his chin and started to pull the mask away. It made a puckering sound as rubber separated from skin. The skin underneath was dry, splotchy, and beet red.

"My dad is coming back," Nathan squeaked.

"He got your tickets?"

Nathan nodded.

Both boy and bull glanced up at the stairs. Nathan saw no sign of his dad.

"Well, mind if I sit next to you till we can figure it out?"

Yes! Nathan very much minded. The bull started sitting down in the seat that was supposed to be his dad's. Nathan stared in watchful terror as the man got comfortable and the two people with him settled into the seats on his left. Nathan looked at the stairs again. What if his dad missed them because the man was blocking Nathan. If he didn't see him, he might've just walked on by. Walked further down the stairs and—

Nathan stood.

"Whoa, no you're good, you're good," said the masked bull.

Nathan was not good. He thought about skirting past the man's knees, but they bucked against the seat in front of him and he'd have to leap over them to make a run for it. He turned the other way. The aisle was mostly open. He started making his way across it. *Dad lost me. He didn't see me. Have to find him. Have to—*

He broke into the aisle on the other side and

bolted up the stairs. He dodged past people carrying food and drink and talking in excited, roaring voices. When he got up top, he looked left and then right and decided to run right. That had to be the direction his dad was in, didn't it?

Twice he thought he saw him. In a stadium this size, everyone looked almost the same. Except for the few people wearing special outfits—or masks—most people were unrecognizable. Nathan darted around a line of people waiting for food and kept running. He looked back only once to make sure he didn't miss his father.

When he did, he saw the same man with the bull face walking not far behind him.

No!

He ran faster. The man stared at him as he went, then tapered off into one of the lines. His bull face tilted up at the menu. Nathan didn't slow. He had to find his dad. *He's here somewhere*, he thought. He kept running. Kept running. Kept—

"Not on my watch!" A man shouted up ahead and Nathan heard the distinctive sound of shattered glass.

"Ayyy what was that for?"

"Fuck, my bad man…"

"Georgie, let's getchu another drink."

The voices came into view as Nathan passed a group of maybe four of five men and one woman. She looked right at home with them though. They all wore the same thing, but instead of the red jerseys everyone else had on they were wearing blue. When Nathan walked past they all turned to him. One of the men lifted the remaining half of a shattered beer stint and tilted it Nathan's way.

"Getreadytoloosefuckers," he slurred like it was all a single word.

It sounded foreign to Nathan.

The man made a move to stand up. Nathan tuned into the sharp glass in his hand and the thin lines of blood cascading down his balled fist. His eyes widened and he stumbled back. The man lowered the glass and grimaced. Nathan ran.

He wasn't sure how far he ran, but eventually the people started tapering off. More of them were in the stands by now. Nathan kept running, but his run slowly became a jog, then a walk, and then he sat down in the middle of the concession area and just started crying. He was never going to find his dad. He'd left him here. Here of all places! And he'd never see him again. He buried his face in his hands and sobbed.

A security guard found him and made an announcement over the loud speaker. "Will the parent of Nathan Cooley please come to the top of section 143." It took all but ten minutes for his dad to make his way over there and find them. When they did, Nathan ran into his dad's arms and cried into his jersey.

"Thank you," he said to the security guard. Then, to Nathan he said, "We'll talk about this."

But they never did. When they were done with the security guard, they said goodbye and thank you to her and went straight back to their seats. Nathan tugged at his dad's arm and begged him to not take him back there. He thought about the bull's face, and about the shattered glass in that man's bloodied hand. The woman with her boobs out and her nachos high. The guard at the front with her wispy hair and the one who'd found him who smelled like burnt burgers.

"I don't wanna," he said. He said it again and again and again as they made their way down to their seats. But still his dad brought them back, squeezed them past bull-face and his companions, and plopped them down into their spots.

"Just till halftime," he told him.

Nathan didn't even know what that meant. Was that still gonna be an hour? Two hours? How long did these games go? Nathan never watched them when they were home together. His dad put them on, and his mom usually made a dip or nachos or something else tasty that Nathan wanted to be around for. Sometimes he thought he knew what was going on on screen, but most of the time he didn't. He didn't care to know, either, and he especially didn't care to know now. But they sat there until halftime and then made their way out the stadium together.

They never talked about that moment again, not for years anyway. Nathan was in college, home for the summer the next time it was brought up. The Red Wings were playing again, and his dad had secured tickets. He looked at Nathan from across the dinner table and said, "I'm gonna ask you this time. Wanna go?"

He did not. But now, Nathan was twenty. He was old enough to know that sometimes you do things for other people because they want them, and sometimes it has nothing to do with you. "Sure," he said. "When is it?"

"Two nights from now."

He looked from his dad to his mom. She kept her head down and out of it. She was remembering the game all those years ago.

"I'm down," Nathan repeated. "We'll stay till halftime?"

It was a joke, but he saw real fear ignite in his dad's eyes. Did he regret asking him already? He shook his head and gave a little chuckle.

"You were way too young to go back then," he said. "I should've known."

Should've known what? Even now, Nathan wasn't too sure what that meant.

"Say, do me a solid," his dad said. "When you have kids, don't put 'em in a place they don't wanna be. 'Kay?"

Nathan took another bite of chicken and smiled. He hadn't told his parents yet, but he wasn't sure he ever wanted to have kids. All the same, he said, "I promise, Dad."

Hollie came downstairs a half hour later. Nathan was sitting on the bottom step, facing the front door, and heard her stepping down. He turned and stood up.

"He's fine," she said. "Just needs some time."

Nathan breathed out. "That's good."

Hollie made it to the bottom step and stared at him. He couldn't read what was behind her eyes. Maybe he hadn't been able to for years.

"I'm sorry," she said.

"I am too."

She looked ready to say more but decided against it. "Do you want to walk me out?"

"You're leaving?"

Down the hall, around the bend and into the living room, Eliza and the others were watching the boys wrestle. They were all laughing and the air in the room was hot with joyful energy. *Tyler should be down here*, Nathan thought. Then he thought again. *He doesn't even want to be here...*

"I'll swing by tomorrow night and get them all," she said. "Six work?"

"I'm flexible," said Nathan.

She nodded. When Eliza glanced into the foyer and waved, Hollie said, "I'm heading out. It was nice meeting you all."

Penny and Helen waved too, and Nathan followed Hollie to the door. He opened it and held it out for her.

"Thanks," she said.

He smiled weakly. "Does he need anything else tonight?"

She met his eyes again. "A good time. He needs a good birthday."

Then, she leaned in and wrapped her arms around him. When she hugged him, a rush of memories boiled up to the surface. Nathan thought about long summer nights when they were first getting together, bodies pressed against each other under sheets made sticky with summer heat. Skin against skin, lips against lips. He wrapped his arms around her too and buried his face in her hair. She smelled different than she had back then, but there was still a familiarity to it. When they broke the hug and looked at one another, his first thought was that maybe it was a good thing she was moving away. Maybe you don't move on when the past is in plain sight.

She got in her car and drove off. Nathan stood there as her car rounded the bend and took a deep breath. Then, he walked back inside and closed the door behind him.

No sooner had he stepped inside did one of the boys run up to him.

"Can we have cake soon?" he asked

He looked down at the kid—Adam, this one had to be Adam—and shook his head. "Just a sec," he said. "I want to talk to him first."

13

K *nock knock...*
"Tyler?"
The door squealed as Nathan pushed it open. Inside his room, Tyler didn't look up. He was sitting on his bed with his sketchpad out in front of him. Two pieces of paper were ripped out and tossed to the side. One next to him, still on the bed; the other on the floor beside it. He was drawing on a third with the same black fountain pen he always used. He drew a circle in the center of the page and then ripped it out of the sketchbook, tossed it with the others.

"Hey bud, alright if I come in?"

"Sure." His head stayed down.

Nathan crept to the side of the bed and slid onto the mattress. "Whatcha doing?"

"Drawing."

"Nice." He peered over at the drawing Tyler had just finished. It showed a square house with a pointy roof and a round drive. There was a car driving down that drive and onto the main road. Up ahead of the car, a huge mess of swirling pen marks lorded over the rest of the page.

"What's this?" He pointed at the inky tornado.

Tyler shrugged. "I dunno."

"What do you think it is?"

"Don't know." Tyler had started on a fourth drawing now. It was a collection of round objects scattered across a living room. *Balloons*, thought Nathan. Then, Tyler lifted his pen and drew streamers cascading down the page. They weren't tied to anything, but instead fell from somewhere far off the page.

"I'm sorry you heard all that," said Nathan. He watched his son draw. Neither of them looked up and met each other's eyes. Something about the whole scene made Nathan even sadder. "Your mom and I shouldn't have yelled." Tyler didn't reply. Instead, he ripped the page from the sketchpad and handed it to Nathan. "Is this for me?"

He nodded. "Thank you for the party."

He looked down at the drawing. Underneath some of the balloons, Tyler had scribbled dark shadows. It made them look more three dimensional. A few of them even looked ready to burst from the page, like Nathan could blow on the paper, and confetti like circles would flutter down across the bedspread and the lap of his now six-year-old boy.

"Are these balloons?" he asked.

"Uh huh." Tyler still didn't look up. "But they're full of blood."

Nathan's body went cold. "Full of what?"

"Blood," Tyler repeated. "I'm not sure why."

Nathan held the drawing out in front of him, looked between it and his son. He cleared his throat. "Do you ever know what you're going to draw?"

Tyler shook his head.

"It just comes out of you?"

A nod.

Nathan craned across the bed at Tyler's sketches.

He plucked one from the bottom of the stack. "What's this one?"

The drawing was nothing but a scribbled mess. He thought there was a bed underneath the hurricane of black ink, but it just as soon could've been a porch, or a car, or a desk. He could tell there was a window, and he thought he saw a circular moon resting in the middle of it. Nathan glanced up, not at the drawing but out his own window. The same moon poked out from behind a thin, foggy layer of clouds now.

"That's me," said Tyler.

A pang hit Nathan's chest. "You?"

Another nod. Tyler kept his mouth tight even as he spoke. "Sometimes I just feel like that."

One of the first moments when Nathan truly knew he was a parent was when Tyler was eleven months old. It had been before he could walk, before he could speak, but not before he could make noise. Like most babies, the day Tyler had clapped had been monumental. The look of shock that spread across his little face and the way his round mouth fell open lived on in Nathan's mind long after that moment faded from memory. For weeks after that, all Tyler did was clap. Some nights, when he was particularly rambunctious, Nathan and Hollie would be asleep, desperately clinging to the few fleeting hours of shut eye they got as new parents, only to hear Tyler from the other room, performing to an invisible crowd around his crib. The first time it happened, Nathan sprinted to the nursery. When he saw that his son was clapping and smiling to himself in the dark room, he had thought that maybe everything was going to be alright. They weren't raising a creature who could be harmed around every corner, but instead a little boy who liked to smile, clap, and wave his hands as his daddy reached into the crib and picked him up. He swaddled him in his arms and cooed him back to sleep. He stayed there for almost twenty minutes before Hollie came into the room, put a hand on his shoulder, and asked him back to bed. *In a minute,* he told her. *Be right there.* But it was much longer than a minute before he was willing to put Tyler back down. He kept thinking about those claps, about that smile, and just how proud of himself Tyler had looked. *I'm raising that*, Nathan thought. I'm a part of that. In that moment, he *got* his son. He understood what they were doing together.

As he looked down at Tyler now, he was no longer sure where that clapping infant had gone. Tyler's eyes were hooded and rimmed in shadow. His mouth was as tight as his hand was around his pen. Nathan used to think the hardest moment for any parent was when they looked at their child and started to see a stranger. It happened with teens; that's what all the books Hollie suggested told him. Landry told him it would happen to everyone. Hell, Nathan knew that it would because it happened to him. His parents stopped seeing him as their son but instead as a nuisance, as just another teenager, then as an adult, then as someone they loved but from a distance.

Nobody prepared Nathan to look at his six-year-old and know him in a way he never should have.

He knew the slope of his shoulders as his hand stretched across the next piece of paper. He knew the haunted look in his eyes, the bloodshot irises, the tear-stained cheeks. When was the last time Tyler had a full night's sleep? When was the last time Nathan had? His son was six but held the same weight Nathan felt now. *You worry for two these days*...but what if his son had been worrying enough for them all?

I did that, Nathan thought. *We did that. We...*

He placed a hand around Tyler and pulled him into his chest. He kept the drawing trapped in his left hand.

"We all feel like that sometimes," he said. "I know I do."

Tyler's hand kept fidgeting across the sketchpad. He leaned into his father, brushed his head against his chest, but he didn't stop drawing. Nathan looked down. Tyler's eyes were closed, and silent tears collected at their edges. His shoulders shuddered up and down, but his hand kept moving.

"And I know it's hard...to hear your mom and I fight like that. It's 'cause we love you, bud. We love you so so much."

Tyler's hand gathered speed and flew across the paper. Nathan watched as Tyler's squiggly lines connected into two sloping shoulders.

"And I know I don't do the right things all the time. But you have to understand—"

One of the sloping shoulders ended at a sharp point halfway down the page.

A body, he's drawing a body.

"—It isn't easy to figure this all out. I wish I got to see you more, kiddo. Really, I do. Heck, I wish I could see you every day. I wanna be there to drop you off at school and pick you up at the end of the day. I wanna cook dinner with you and take you to the park. We can even go down to the river together. Grandpa and I used to skip rocks together. Did he ever tell you that? Maybe we could do that too. We'd get KFC or Wendy's or something else that's real bad for you but tastes like it should be real good, and just go skip rocks and explore together. Maybe we could—"

The pen lifted back to the other shoulder. He had

already drawn one, normal sized arm. This time, the shoulder sloped further, a waterslide that was too steep for the little kids and just right for the big ones. It became longer, longer still, until the page ended, and Tyler had drawn a bit of the line onto his light green bedspread. He had picked that bedspread out all by himself. He loved it.

"—Oh, I don't know. We could do it all. But I know your mom wants to do those things too. And really, bud, we tried. We really really tried." Tyler's breath hiked and Nathan squeezed him tighter. "We just weren't ready to love each other forever. I wasn't ready for that. I thought I was. But I wasn't. I am now." *With you*, he wanted to add. *With you, I'm ready for forever.*

Only he couldn't say that, because suddenly he was staring at the drawing his son was creating. Tyler's eyes were still closed, his breath came out in sharp, sputtering gasps. Still breathing though, still breathing. Tyler lifted his hand and drew a small circle above the shoulders, then a long, thin line atop that. The wide brim of a shadowy hat. He picked up the pen again and went to his next location. The hand. He's going for the hand. Then, Tyler's hand spasmed and he dropped the pen. He fell into Nathan's side and his eyes fluttered open.

His face was a deep shade of blood red.

"Tyler? Hey, hey it's alright."

Tyler's lips parted. They were slightly blue around the edges. His eyes grew wide. He turned and stared at Nathan, and he saw the boy try to breathe in.

Try—and fail.

His face was growing brighter now, the blue was starting to spread. Tyler reached out an arm and it spasmed across his papers. His current drawing flew across the room and landed right outside the closet. It faced upward.

The Lop-Sided man stared back at them.

"Tyler?" Nathan stood and pulled his son off the bed. *Get him into a standing position. Get behind him. He's choking on something...something that...something that isn't—*

The lop-sided man...

No.

The bedroom door flung shut. Nathan turned and watched it hit the wall. Then he heard a lock click in the knob. He still held his son, who was still struggling to breathe. *Keep fighting,* he told him. *Keep fighting.*

The lights flickered and Nathan looked up. No, this isn't happening. He set Tyler back on the bed and ran for the door. He jiggled the knob, but something was locking it from the outside. He turned the lock back and forth, but nothing happened. "Hello!" he shouted. "Help! Help!" Someone would hear him. "*Hello!!*" He could hear them. Music was playing lightly. Maybe they'd all forgotten about them up here.

They won't heaaaarr youuuu Natthaaaannn...

He turned slowly toward the closet. As he did, the flickering light went out and the room was thrown into darkness. The moon cast a dim beam over the bed where Tyler was still struggling for breath but sitting up now. There was color in his face again, and it looked like whatever had gripped him was letting go. *Naaathaaaannn...*

Now, it turned its attention toward him.

The closet door popped open an inch, and a dark shadow spilled out like an inky stain. Smoke billowed near the foot of the door, and Nathan wondered for the first time not what was living in that closet, but where they had come from. Where did that closet lead? He waited for a hand, surely something was pushing the door open, but it didn't come. Instead, the door kept swinging. He stared in terror, legs drowned in concrete, unable to move, as the door opened halfway, then fully, and, like a giant, cavernous maw, the entire room seemed to silently roar.

Then, a figure stepped out.

Not the one he expected though.

Nathan watched as *he* walked out of the closet—only, it wasn't him, exactly. They had the same hairline, the same average height. His build was that of a Nathan from yesteryear, before he got back to the gym and started working out. Before Tyler. Before the showers. Before Hollie and her stupid, stupid soaps. He wore a red button up shirt, the same color Tyler's face had been, with a black tie that made him look like a Chili's employee who got the uniform just slightly wrong. His slacks were too tight around the waist. They were clothes Nathan used to own. He was sure of it.

But this Nathan had only one eye staring back at him.

The other socket was empty, a window to a hollow skull where a thin tendril of smoke rose. With the smoke came the faint wriggle of an earthworm crawling out of this Nathan's empty socket. The worm inched its way out, then turned and tunneled up this Nathan's nose. Nathan thought for a moment he felt it in him as well.

Then, this Nathan lifted an arm. The hand on the other end flopped forward, wrist limp. A white bone jutted out from that wrist and pointed accusatorially skyward.

Nathan stumbled back into the door. On the other

side he thought he felt banging. And...could he hear his name? The door handle jiggled.

"What are you?" he asked.

The other Nathan's head lolled to the side. His outstretched hand morphed into a point and shot a dagger his direction. *Thisssss....this is meeee...*

"No." He shook his head.

"Nathan!?"

This time he heard Eliza's voice clearly. She was just on the other end of the door. But she didn't know what was in here with them. She didn't know.

He glanced down. Smoke pooled at his feet.

"What is that, Nathan? Open the door!"

Then, a weaker voice from across the room... "Daddy?"

Both Nathan's turned to their son.

"Tyler!" He ran for the bed, and as he did, the other Nathan lunged forward, not at the boy, but at Nathan. He dodged out of the monster's way and dove for Tyler's bed. He grabbed him and Tyler buried his face in his chest. His eyes still peeked out though, stared at the other man in the room with them.

Naaaathaaaannn...

"D-da-daddy..."

"It's okay," he said.

But his heart was beating so fast the words came out uneven. He looked at the window. Smash it open? Get them out of there? Somehow, he knew it wouldn't work like that. The Lop-Sided man wanted them in here, and so they would stay.

The other Nathan leaned against the door now as Eliza called from the other side, "Nathan is that you? Nathan open the door!"

Not me, thought Nathan. *Not me, not me, not me.*

He gripped Tyler closer as the other Nathan started to transform.

I'vveeee waaaiiiittteed for youuuuuu...

The first thing to fall was his outstretched hand. The snapped bone vanished, sank back into his wrist, and as it did, the skin of his arm started to melt, stretching out like taffy onto the ground. He opened his mouth to scream, and specks of dirt came out. A living worm and a dead spider's carcass fell out. The worm moved aimlessly at the thing's feet. Then, he grew taller. His feet stretched into amorphous shadows, and his skin started vanishing into the dark. His skin seemed almost to pull to either side. The other eye snapped out of its socket and rolled onto the floor. The sight of his own eye inching closer and closer till it settled at the foot of the bed was enough to turn Nathan's stomach.

Naaaathaaaan... His name echoed, and both he and Tyler shivered. Nathan looked away. When he dared look out again, the thing before them was barely visible in the dark. The moonlight revealed him. The Lop-Sided man's hand was still outstretched, only longer now, and as it tumbled through the darkness, Nathan ducked down, holding Tyler even tighter. He wasn't sure the boy could breathe. He would have to, though. For just a little while longer.

I'm sorry, Tyler. So, so sorry...

I'vveeee waaaiiiittteed for youuuuuu to finaalllyyy come...

Shadows dripped from the demonic face. The expression was dead. There was no mouth, no teeth like his nightmare; instead, there were only eyes. Two glowing yellow orbs that seared like dying stars into Nathan's own. It tilted its head down; the brim of its wide hat covered one of its eyes. The other stared on.

Tyler shook in his arms. "D-daddy?" His voice came out as a cough.

Give hiiiiim to meeeeee. Give hiiiim...

"No!" Nathan sputtered the word out. His mouth felt dry and chalky. "No!"

I will leeaaaavvee when I haaaave hiiiim.

"You won't!"

I wiiiiiillllll...

The Lop-Sided man reached out with his long arm and the hand settled for a second on Tyler's shoulder. The boy ripped it free, and when it came away, there was a hole in his shirt. The skin underneath was splotchy and red. Tears dripped from the corners of his eyes. Nathan pulled him back further.

"No!"

"Daddy!"

They were up against the wall now. That arm kept stretching though. In seconds it would be on them. On Tyler. On—

"NO!" Nathan, still holding his son against his chest, reached around to the boy's nightstand. It was a new nightstand, no sign of being crushed only weeks before.

And inside there was a gun.

The hilt glistened against the moonlight, and if Nathan had been watching his son's eyes, he would've seen them widen. He wasn't looking at his son's expression, though. The six-year-old watched his daddy raise the gun up, and then a moment later he felt the cold, metallic kiss of the revolver against his temple.

"You won't take my son from me!"

"D-daddy..."

The Lop-Sided man crept forward. There was still banging on the front door. They would get it open soon, wouldn't they? What then? What would happen then? The monster's long arm fell. It hit the bed and more smoke rose between Nathan and the Lop-Sided man. It took another lumbering step forward, and Nathan saw its whole body ripple in the moonlight, like a shadow might fizzle when the light hit it just right. For a second, it seemed almost to vanish, like it wasn't there at all. Then it reappeared, closer this time, and Nathan was staring into those yellow eyes and wishing for death.

Give himmmm to meeee...Naaathaaaann he is allll I want...

He's all I want! thought Nathan. He pressed the barrel of the gun further into Tyler's temple. He wouldn't shoot him. He wouldn't. Just tempt the monster. Tempt him down. Make him step back.

"Naaaathaaaannn!"

Eliza's voice was shrill. The bedroom door seemed ready to shoot off its hinges. Do it, he thought. Do it now. See what's been haunting us. Help me save my son.

Youuuuu caaannn't saaaveee him...

"I can!"

"Nathan?" shouted Eliza.

The Lop-Sided man lowered his head and a low, lonely chuckle rose through the air around them and spiraled up. As it did, the smoke kicked up from the monster's feet, and soon he was covered. When the smoke cleared, the Lop-Sided man had taken another shape. He was Nathan again, but this time he was whole. He wore the same flannel he wore now. The same straight legged jeans, with a frayed hem on the left leg. All that was left of the monster was the mis-shapen arm. It still lay long, stretched onto the ground.

Caaaannn you...?

"No! I can!" He shut his eyes and turned toward Tyler. "I'm sorry. I'm sorry I brought you here."

"Daddy…"

Tyler was crying now—no, Nathan was crying. Tyler was breathing, steady and strong. He fought against Nathan's grip, but the other Nathan stepped forward and closed the space between them. He reached up his long arm and bent it back the way a scorpion does when it's about to strike. His hand was as wide as Tyler's head. He wanted to crush it, squeeze it, end him and take him from Nathan forever.

"You won't do it—"

Naaaathaaaan….

"DADDY!!"

He heard more footsteps clamber down the hallway, but he didn't hear Eliza at the door. If she was still there, still calling, it was with wasted breath.

"Tyler," he breathed out. "I'm so sorry." *Should've left him at home. Should've never brought him here. This was never a home. Never anything close to—*

The window flung open.

Nathan turned as the screen fell into the room and a strong gust of bitter air smacked against the two of them. *That's the bedtime breeze,* he thought. *It can't getcha here. It won't getcha.* He pushed the revolver deeper into his son's wriggling head. "Don't let the bedtime breeze getcha, kid. Don't let him—him…"

It was the Lop-Sided man in front of them again, and his arm was just inches away. So close. Too close. Too— His arm grabbed Tyler's head, pulled his neck backwards.

"NO!" screamed Nathan, and the sound Tyler sent into the night air was deafening.

Smoke poured from his steaming body. Nathan gripped him tighter. *I won't let go. I won't let go. He's mine. Mine! Miiiinnneee!* The demon's other arm grabbed at his shoulder and he felt it start to tear at his shirt, piercing through his skin. There was no more time to think. This had to be over.

He pulled the gun's trigger. Two shots fired.

The night, with its bedtime breeze, went still.

14

E liza Shepherd was not the worrying sort. In college, she remembered staying up late to study for an exam only once during her first year. It had been an Art History exam, and she'd just about failed almost every test leading up to the final. The best she could hope for now in the class was a C, maybe a B if she pulled out some magic. *This final will be worth a third of your total grade...*That was what Professor Sandia said. That was what kept her up well past four then five in the morning. By the time she got to the exam room, her eyes were half hooded and her heart had that low sort of beating it only got when it was too tired, the kind of beating you felt pushing against your rib cage and other organs. She never stayed up that late worrying again.

Tonight, she was worried for Nathan's sake.

She glanced nervously in the direction of the staircase. "I should check on them," she told Penny, who was sitting cross-legged on the couch next to her. A few of the boys had put on Pixar's Chicken Little. It was at the part now where Chicken Little was discovering a "piece" of the fallen sky and taking it home. For the most part, the boys were silent. Some of them had drooping eyelids, but she knew they wouldn't dare fall asleep before the cake was cut. And then the sugar from that would hype them all back up to eleven for at least another hour after that. Besides, they were young now; there was nothing worse when you were young than falling asleep first at a sleepover.

"They're fine," Penny said. "Just let him do this."

"I know I just—"

I worry.

That was when she heard the loud, frantic banging of fists against a door. She and Penny looked up. Behind them, Helen, who had been putting leftover cans of Sprite back in the drawers of Nathan's fridge, shot up so fast she felt each vertebra crack individually across her spinal line. She groaned audibly behind them.

And then they heard the screams.

"Hello!"

It was Nathan's voice. Eliza turned and ran for the staircase.

"Eliza, wait!" She wasn't sure if it was Penny or Helen who shouted at her, but she was halfway up the stairs and out of sight when they did. She kept running.

"Help! Help!"

Oh God, what was going on?

"Hello!!"

Nathan's voice took on a shrill quality that she almost couldn't recognize as his. There was something cartoonish about the way he screamed from behind the door. First door on the right...it was vibrating softly in the darkened hallway. She grabbed at its handle and tried to force it open. When it didn't budge, she gave the whole thing a yank, but the door wasn't meant to go that way. She knew that. She heard more footsteps following her. Helen climbed the top step. Penny would still be with the other boys.

Keep them watching Chicken Little, Eliza thought. *The sky's not falling yet. Don't make them worry it might be.*

"Nathan!" she called. *Unlock the damn door, Nathan.*

She thought she heard Tyler crying inside. As she did, something dark and inky started pooling out from the gap between the bottom of the door and the floor. It billowed up and out once through the small gap, and Eliza started to cough. She kicked a bit of it away, and the whole cloud dissipated. The smoke carried no scent, but she wrinkled her nose nonetheless.

She looked at Helen, who shook her head briefly.

"What is that, Nathan? Open the door!"

She hit the door in its center. Then, she felt a heavy object standing against the wood on the other side. "Nathan, is that you? Nathan, open the door!" But if it was him, he didn't make a move toward the door handle. Eliza jiggled it again, some desperate part of her who was certain she could get it unlocked if she kept trying. She felt the whole handle start to fall loose. What would happen if it fell out? She would lose access to the room entirely, wouldn't she?

More smoke billowed out the bottom of the door.

The small cracks on the side and top seeped minute amounts of the black fog. Eliza coughed as it shrouded the room.

"What's going on?" asked Helen.

Eliza shook her head.

"Is something on fire?"

But no, she was sure that wasn't the case. This smoke didn't smell like that. It didn't carry any smell, in fact. It was like someone had dip dyed dry ice before watching it work its magic and sent up an ominous black haze as the result. Where would Nathan have gotten dry ice? What was coming from Tyler's room?

Then, she heard Tyler's first audible word.

"...*Daddy...?*"

Eliza's stomach twisted and she threw her entire body against the door. There was a child in there, barely six years old. Whatever was happening, whatever this smoke was...it wasn't good.

Penny's head appeared in the smoke behind Helen. Her arms were waving through the space around her. "What the—" she stopped short and Eliza soon saw why.

All of the other boys were following her, curious where the adults had gone, probably, but just a few steps behind. A few of them stared up at the smokey haze through the room. One looked down and pointed at the bulging billow near Eliza's feet. Eliza turned to Penny.

"Get them down," she whispered through a cough.

"What's going on?" asked Penny.

Nathan answered from inside the bedroom. "NO!"

His shout sent chills racing down Eliza's back. "Nathan!"

But he didn't seem to hear her. She rattled against the door, and in her periphery, she saw one of the boys flinch back. *Good*, she thought. *Go back downstairs. Get away from whatever this is. We'll figure it out and let you know when it's safe to come back upstairs and then, only then—*

"Naaaathaaannn!"

Then, as if in response to her shout, she heard Tyler's voice carry up in that sort of scream only a child was truly capable of. "DADDY!!"

The hallway went silent.

Eliza held fast to the door handle. The other boys were still except for their coughing fits from the haze.

And then, shortly after, there were the gunshots.

The first one shook Eliza from the doorknob. She jumped back, fell into Helen, and turned rapidly to the others. The second shot was firing as she said, "Get them away!"

"Eliza..." said Penny.

"Go!"

"Someone call 9-1-1," said Helen.

"I've got it." Penny dug in her pocket for her phone. "You get the kids."

"Come on boys," said Helen. "Nothing to see here. Nothing to—"

"Is Tyler okay?" one of them asked.

Eliza went to respond, but what could she say to that? She heard a click on the other end of the door. The lock. The lock was turning.

She flew to the doorknob and pulled back against it to hold it in place. Something tugged at the other end, but she pulled back harder.

"Tyler will be fine," said Helen. "Come on."

"Hello—yes, I'm on...Yes, uh, there have been two gunshots fired in the house..."

"Eliza?"

Nathan's voice was sleepy on the other end of the door, almost like he'd just woken up a few minutes ago from the kind of hardy nap that only comes when a power nap goes wrong. Fifteen minutes becomes hours. The world slips away for that godforsaken time.

"Eliza open the door. There's...there's a problem."

*I know that...*she thought. *The problem is you have a gun. Where did you get a gun, Nathan? Why was it in your kid's room? Why did he scream right before you shot it? Why isn't he talking now?*

When Nathan yanked again on the door, Eliza eased up on her end. The door slid half an inch from its frame, and Eliza caught the metallic smell of fresh blood. Nathan slid his hand against the door, fingers reaching through the opening, searching for the handle. In his other hand, she noticed the gun still swinging. Her eyes widened with terror. No! She threw the door closed, giving no notice to where his fingers were. She slammed it shut and crunched his pointer and index finger on his left hand in the process.

"*Agh!*" he screamed.

The door popped back open and he pulled his fingers back. Through the crack, Eliza saw him lift the gun, then aim it toward her. She pulled the door shut again and, with all the force she could manage, kept it that way.

Nathan rammed his body against the door.

"Ahhh!" His scream was almost animal. Eliza shut her eyes and bent her neck backwards. She could still smell it through the door—that tangy, raw stench of freshly spilled blood. *Tyler...*

Her lips started to quiver. "N-na-nathan..."

"No!" Then, he slammed his body into the door again and she felt him try to turn the handle. She tightened herself against it, pulling back with steady force. Even so, he was stronger than her. His pull lifted the door from its frame for half a second before she was able to overcorrect and station it back in. Her arms shook and across her forehead, prickles of sweat started puckering up.

Stay in there...he has to stay in there. She craned her neck sideways and glanced down the stairs. How long would the police take? How long would she stay here?

From the other side of the door she heard Nathan mutter, "You did this..."

Who was he talking to?

"You...you..."

Oh fuck, he's lost it. She leaned her forehead against the door and placed a foot on either side of the door frame. She slid down the door and steadied herself somewhere halfway down its length. As she did, she heard another gunshot ring out. She shut her eyes again. Who was left for him to shoot? Tyler made no noise when the gun fired. He wasn't there to hear it anymore—she just knew it. Another shot rang overhead and the whole door rattled. Eliza glanced up and saw a hole in the door a few feet above where she was bent over. He'd shot through the door and hit the wall behind her. Little flecks of debris fell on her from where the door was ripped open.

He's gonna shoot me, too...

No, he couldn't. She had to stay strong. Keep him here. Make sure he doesn't hurt anyone else. She thought for a fleeting, frantic moment, *where is the man I had over for wine night?*

"ELIZA LET ME OUT!"

He didn't even sound like himself. She felt like crying, but her body was too tense to let tears out. The voice coming from the other side of the door was dark, twisted, grizzly. She shut her eyes and tried not to imagine herself getting shot while she stayed here. The door handle rattled, Nathan's body slammed against the frame, but she stayed put. She had to.

Nathan slammed against the door again.

"Eliza! Eliza! Eliza!"

Even her name felt foreign on his tongue. Her vision misted from gathering waterworks, but she pulled tighter against the door. If he sent another bullet her way, let it hit her stomach. Somewhere she could keep holding on. There were kids downstairs. They had to stay safe.

Like Tyler.

No. No, no, no...

No gunshot came.

Maybe he was out of ammo.

"He's still in here!" Nathan cried into the lonely night. Eliza tried to shut the words out, shut her eyes tight the way a little kid does when they don't want to see what monsters look in the dark, but still they cut through. "He's still in here! He's still here!"

When the police arrived, Penny let them in and rushed them upstairs. Eliza still stood in the hall, forehead against the door, hand pulling back against the knob, though really, she hadn't been pulling with the same pressure. Nathan seemed to step away from the door almost twenty minutes ago, and now all she could hear from him was the occasional mutter or tearful breath. She never made out the muttering, but she presumed to know what he was saying.

He's still in here...He's still here.

The first officer was a stout man with a full mustache and a balding head. Tiny patches of peach fuzz assembled around the crown of his head. But his eyes were kind and his hands warm as they gently peeled Eliza off the door by her shoulders and helped her stand up.

"Thank you," she whispered.

He nodded, then turned to the door. "He's in there?"

"Y-yes."

Another cop came up the stairs then, this one a

blonde woman who was wider in the shoulders and larger in the hips than the man who'd helped Eliza. "Harris," said the first, "Help her to the others."

"Roger. Come on." Her voice had a heavy New England accent. "You've done well." She patted Eliza on the back as she led her down the stairs. Eliza turned back around just as the first officer entered the room.

"Nathan," she heard him say before the door was peeled all the way open. He entered with his gun threatening forward. "Drop the gun. Let's talk."

Then, she heard nothing. She and Officer Harris rounded the corner downstairs and Helen ran up and offered her a hug. She accepted it with a wave of gratitude. Warmth simmered in her stomach, and she bent into Helen's shoulder.

"Penny's with the boys," she said. "Oh, God, you didn't see, did you?"

No. But she knew. Tyler...*he's still in here*...that fresh smell of blood. Officer Harris clapped a hand on either woman's shoulder. She said, "What's done is done. Let's get you safely out of here. Then we'll discuss what happened."

They joined the others. Officer Harris held them in the far corner of the kitchen, out of sight of the staircase or the front door, for a long time. She didn't ask any questions, but she didn't stop them from talking. The boys weren't asking anything right now, and for that Eliza was thankful. What was she going to say when they started asking? Hell, there were kids here. Kids! They weren't going to just forget this ever happened.

I'm not going to forget it ever happened...

She slumped down into one of Nathan's dining chairs

and rested her chin in the palm of her right hand. When she closed her eyes, she tried not to see Tyler's brain mushing out the side of his skull. Whenever she did, her mind turned it to a living matter and the pieces started wriggling across the carpet, trying to piece themselves back together. They would drown in the pool of blood soaking the bedroom floor before they could get there.

There were four officers there in total. Harris stayed with them, but the other three—all men, all middle aged, all dangling Glock 17 pistols from their belts—went up to Nathan in the bedroom. Soon, Eliza heard him start to scream. The screams grew closer, and she perked up. Harris held her down with a calming hand on the back of her neck.

"He's still there!" Nathan shouted. "Still there!"

Eliza flinched and next to her, Penny lowered her head. Helen stared on, but her eyes were large and watery.

Still there? Who was still there?

They dragged Nathan out the front door and closed it behind them. She wasn't sure how long they stayed there, tucked away in their little corner, but it felt like forever before Officer Barnes, the man who first came up to help Eliza off the door, came up to them.

"How is everyone doing, let's start there?"

Nobody jumped to respond. A few of the boys looked between Officer Barnes and the three women they'd been with all night, but still stayed silent.

"Here," said Harris. She was looking at Eliza. "You live nearby?"

"Next door."

She nodded. "Let's go there. I think we all need to get out of here. Forensic analysts will be here shortly, and it would do better for us all to talk in a more… neutral space."

Eliza nodded and stood from her chair. "Let me just call my husband." She did, and when she did, she broke down. It took almost five minutes before she got out enough of what happened to ask him to bring everyone over. He agreed it was for the best, and after that she led the procession from Nathan's house to hers. When he opened the door, Ethan embraced her and for a moment she could pretend they were fine, that *everything* was fine. That melted away when he pulled away and turned to greet both officers as well as the other women and the kids. He ushered them inside. Another car would be pulling up to Nathan's house shortly, Barnes told them. Forensics experts would determine the cause of death and pair it with what they all said tonight to piece together what happened.

I can tell you what happened, Eliza thought. *It's a story you won't like.*

She closed the door behind them all.

———

"Thank you…for answering those." Harris sat back in the chair across from Eliza and set her pencil down. Her notepad was open across the kitchen table. For the last thirty minutes, maybe longer if the way Eliza felt was true reality, Harris had asked her about the night. How she had known Nathan, how tonight was supposed to go, what happened right before things went south. For most of her questions, Eliza had flimsy answers at best. She hadn't known Nathan long, and though they were getting close, she thought that maybe there had always been more distance between them than she realized. *I didn't know he had a gun...no, Tyler never seemed scared of him. He loved his dad...I thought he seemed very happy.* She told them about the night terror, but only because what else did she have to offer them? The way Harris jotted down the statement looked as if she was already discrediting it. Lots of people had night terrors; very few shot at their six-year-old son as a result.

"Course," said Eliza. She sniffled in, though her nose, and eyes, and entire face felt brittle at this point. The tears she shed in Nathan's house had run her river dry. "What...what did they find in there?"

Harris stood now. Her partner was under the arch that led from the hallway to the kitchen. He shook his head lightly in the candlelight. Harris turned back to her.

"Not good," she said.

Eliza nodded. That was more of an answer than she expected. It was more than she wanted, too. He's gone. He shot his son and lost his mind. She slammed her fist against the table. God, she should've seen it. Why hadn't she seen it?

"Mrs. Shepherd." Harris rested a gentle hand on her shoulder. She realized she was shaking.

"Sorry. I—He was a good kid."

Harris and Barnes both nodded. It was Barnes who spoke then. "They always are."

Then, the two of them left. Ethan was waiting behind them, and he exchanged a few words with the cops as he let them pass. The others were all in the living room. The other women had been questioned first. They had waited to start until the other boys had been picked up. Spencer's mom came and got them all. Hollie Smart had been called to a different location. It wasn't a good idea to bring her here. When his mom did get here, Spencer dove into her arms. He didn't cry the way Eliza thought he might, and he didn't squirm away from her hug. There was something highly adult about the little man as he rubbed his mom's back and told her, "I'm okay. I'm okay mom." Eliza thought his mom would be inconsolable until she saw that. She'd been crying even before they let her in. It was only Spencer who sucked her tears back in and brought out a genuine smile.

Something about it made Eliza think of Tyler and his sparkler. How long ago had that summer day been? When had it all gone so cold?

She thanked them and took Spencer and the other boys to her car. She exchanged words with Officer Harris in the driveway and the two women shook hands before she got in the car and drove off. The minivan faded into the shrouded night.

Eliza joined the other women in her living room. Neither of them spoke when she walked in. What was there to say? The night was over now, and the party had come and gone. Both of them looked exhausted. Eliza felt the same inside.

War, she thought. *We look like war.*

Officer Barnes stood before them in the foyer. "Thank you ladies. You did a brave thing calling us. We—" he looked at officer Harris, "We will reach out for any further questioning."

Penny sat up. "What about Tyler?"

Eliza and Helen both looked up at the officers. Barnes looked to Harris, then shook his head again, the same way he had moments earlier in the kitchen.

"He's dead."

Then he dropped his head and let out a sigh. Penny didn't ask for further details. Helen didn't either. Eliza wanted to but found it impossible to shape what she still needed to know. He was dead. That little boy with the effervescent smile and head of gold spun curls was dead.

"Thank you both," said Ethan. "I'll walk you out."

And so, he did. The door stayed propped open behind them, and the heavy gust of late November air sent chills down Eliza's back. Ethan returned and locked the door behind him. He offered both women the chance to stay with them tonight. Neither took it. Helen was picked up first; Penny waited for her before driving herself home. In the silence of the driveway, Penny hugged Eliza for a good long while. When she pulled away, she still held her arms and said, "I didn't think he could do that."

Eliza shook her head. "Neither did I."

The two women parted ways and Eliza shut the door behind her.

She practically fell into Ethan's arms. It was there she finally shattered. "I know," he whispered into her hair, "I know. It's gonna be alright...it's over. It's finally over."

Over?

She still sobbed but managed to crane her neck to the side. The back of her head rubbed against Ethan's cheek now. Her eyes faced out their window and stared directly at Nathan's house. A light still shone from a second story window. She shut her eyes tightly again and buried her face in her husband's shoulder. *Over?* she asked herself again. Then, unwillingly, Nathan's final, desperate calls came to mind. *He's still in there...still there...*

She took a deep breath and looked up.

"I feel like a wreck," she said, and a wet laugh sputtered out of her.

"You don't look it." The way he smiled made Eliza

almost forget they had problems, that just a few days ago she had been working the courage up to end things. She would still find that courage, just not yet. "Come on. Let's go to bed."

And so, she followed him. With all the early tenderness of their freshly budding relationship, she went with him to bed. They didn't make love. They didn't hold each other close. By now they were well past that. The last time they made love was almost five months ago, and it had felt like a duty on both ends rather than an act of any true passion. But, knowing he was there, just an arm's length away, Eliza felt she could almost sleep soundly for the night. Just as she was about to fall, she turned her head to the window and her eyes flicked open. That light was off in Nathan's house. She thought that was odd. Hadn't the police left already? But fatigue won against her and the next time her eyes blinked shut, they stayed that way.

DECEMBER

15

The first snow fell on December 14th that year. It was the kind of fresh powder perfect for snow forts and tackle fights—the kind of snow that brushed easily off windshields and frosted windowsills with a Hallmark fluff that looked edible and sweet.

December 14th was also the day of a young six-year-old boy's funeral. Eliza Shepherd sat at home as the service was held, uninvited. As the snow spiraled, she sipped on a glass of warm cocoa. Ethan was out, gone for his last business trip before a two week holiday break that started right before Christmas and ran until January 7th. The house was quiet without him there. Outside, the wind whistled, and a loose rain gutter rattled against the side of the house. When he was back—and when the weather allowed it—she might make Ethan get out on the ladder and fix it. She could do it herself if she wanted, probably even right now. It wasn't cold enough to stop her, and she'd secured the thing before. Instead, she listened to its lonely rattle and flipped through news channels. Surely, somewhere there would be coverage of an event to take her mind of Tyler's body being slowly lowered six feet under.

Six feet.

He was just six years old.

She had known the boy for only a few months. She knew his father for the same amount of time and look how wrong her hunch had turned out about him. Nathan had seemed like a troubled man, but Eliza felt hard pressed to find someone living in the twenty-first century who wasn't troubled at least part-time. She thought again about Ethan and what might be troubling him. Last night, before he'd left for the airport, he had asked her what she wanted to do for the holidays. It had been an odd question. For as long as she could remember, they had been going to her parents' on Christmas and then flying to Omaha where Ethan was from and spending New Year's Eve there with his side of the family. What else would she be planning to do this year? What *she* wanted to do, he'd asked, like she was a queen and they were living in some sort of twisted matriarchy where the monarch in question never asked for any power and sat around feel depressed and stuck all the god damn time.

"I'm fine with whatever, dear," she said. She threw the 'dear' in as a joke. Back when they first got together, the idea of pet names had sickened both of them. Slowly, 'babe' started to feel natural (until the unfortunate day where natural turned patronizing) but for the first year together, even that had been too much. In that time, they had sickened one another by throwing back and forth the cheesiest, most poorly thought out pet names imaginable. Somewhere along the way 'dear' had become their favorite, and it always made them both smile when the name got flung around. That day, however, Ethan didn't crack a smile. He huffed out a breath and looked ready to say more. I dare you...thought Eliza. I fucking dare you. Bring it up. Say you want separate holidays. Say you want separate every-

thing. I do. Oh, I do. He said nothing though and went to wash the dishes in silence. He was picked up by a friend an hour later and driven to the airport.

Troubled, she thought. *Everyone's a little troubled.*

Not everyone shoots their own son, though. There was a thick line in that sandbox.

Eliza caught the CBS news story the same night as everyone else. It had been two nights after Tyler's murder, one night after Nathan's initial imprisonment. *Man shoots son during sixth birthday party.* Somehow, the fact they threw in the number was what hurt the most. Six. Just six. She lowered her head and gripped tightly at the couch cushion hugged against her chest. The telecast missed a few details. They left out Eliza and the other women's names intentionally, and there was no mention of any events leading up to the night. What events had led up to the night? She shook her head and Ethan, who was sitting next to her when the news story came on, reached out a hand and gently placed it on her knee. His touch jolted her, but she didn't brush him away.

Tyler was found with half his head blown right off. Bits of grey brain matter spilled on the floor. Blood pooled around his broken and shattered body. The only fingerprints on the gun had belonged to Nathan. He had purchased it, without a license, from a shop on the east side of town that was now under thorough investigation for both illegal distribution of weaponry and, upon local suspicions, drug trade.They interviewed the owner and the employee who sold Nathan the gun. Both men had little to say, and Eliza got the feeling they were told to wait until a lawyer was present before spilling much else. The interviews were a whole lot of, "Didn't know, sir," and, "He showed me a fake." Pointless, idiotic words. The story lasted maybe five minutes and then was quickly brushed aside in favor of a Pomeranian named Dulce who pulled a missing cat out of a thorny shrub and reunited her with her grieving family—the world *had* to hear about that. Eliza shut off the newscast and went up to bed shortly after.

The hot chocolate had gone cold. Eliza took another sip and then stood from the couch, walked over to the kitchen, and dumped the rest down the sink. She ran the water over her grimy mug and let the rim overflow. Then, she shut it off and walked back to the couch. She stayed there the rest of the day, flipping through channels and scrolling through her endless Instagram feed. She lost herself somewhere in the digital world, so much so that when Ethan called her that night to ask her to check if one of his ties was still hanging in the closet, or if he'd lost it somewhere in between the hotel room and the conference hall, she almost didn't answer. What did it matter if she picked up or not. It wouldn't change the way Ethan felt about her. It wouldn't change the way she felt about him. But she picked up anyway and promptly marched to the second floor, told him the red paisley tie was still hanging in the usual spot and he'd simply forgotten to pack it, and when he asked how her day was, she told him, "Fine. Nothing to report here."

"Good," he said. "I'll be home in three days."

"I know. I—" *I'm excited to see you, I miss you already, I wish you were here...*None of the responses she used to give felt right. "I'll see you then."

There was silence on the other end. Then: "Eliza, don't do this."

"Don't do what?"

"You know..."

"I...we can talk about it when you get home, okay?"

The sigh he let out was low and hollow, and Eliza felt it down the nape of her neck even through the phone. "Alright. I do want to talk about this though. I- babe, I know you're not happy."

Babe.

Oh, Dear, you don't have to call me that. You know, I used to love it, now, I'm not so sure.

"Are you?"

He paused. "I don't think so."

"It's not thinking," she said. "It's feeling."

Then she hung up the phone and burst into tears. If he tried to call back, she didn't know. She had already gone upstairs to take a shower.

When he got home, they would talk. There would be one final conversation. It wouldn't end in blows or shouts or lashing tongues waving back and forth. It wouldn't even end in tears.

In a matter of two days time, both Ethan and Eliza would know they were comfortable with divorce. Ethan would start sleeping on the couch. Eliza would speak to him only when necessary. The divorce was officially filed two weeks after the holidays were over; it wouldn't finalize for months to come.

Nathan Cooley did not know his son was buried that day. None of the officers he saw daily during his stay in Wayne County Jail felt it was pertinent knowledge. *What would it do to an inmate's psyche?* they wondered. Better not to find out.

For his part, Nathan did his best to keep it together. His trial was set for the beginning of January, after the holiday season had wrapped. He was given a lawyer—square jawed and wide shouldered Jefferey Shriver—who visited him once a week to discuss the nature of the case. The day before Tyler's funeral, Shriver had sat across from him in a small soundproof room and asked him for probably the hundredth time, "Did you fire the gun at your son?"

"No," Nathan answered. "I..." he faltered. *It wasn't aimed at him.* "I didn't mean to shoot him."

"But you bought the gun?"

"I did."

"Why?"

Because there was a monster in the closet...because Tyler was defenseless and I am his father and...and...

He shook his head and started to cry. Their session ended shortly after that and Nathan was led back to his holding room, which looked much like the room he supposed he would be spending the rest of his life in after the trial was complete. Seven feet across one way and almost eight the other, it was a nonexistent shoebox of a room with a tiny set of bunk beds tucked away in one corner. Across from them was a small desk with a pull-out chair that hit against the bed frame whenever he pulled it out far enough to slide in. There was a metallic toilet in the opposite corner that was ever so slightly concealed from the holding cell's bars by the fact that the cement wall that separated his cell from the one next-door stretched just enough into his space to create the illusion of privacy. The top of the toilet also functioned as a sink, and the wall it was against had one of those security mirrors welded to the wall.

Nathan laid on the bottom bunk on the evening of his son's funeral and stared at the empty mattress above him. He let his eyes zone in too heavily, until the focus blurred and the white mattress's shape hazed into an empty array of blank color. He held his concentration on it for as long as he could until his eyes and brain and skull throbbed from the pressure. He blinked and his vision righted itself.

He sat up.

"Hey!" he called. The correctional officer stationed in his wing for the day appeared in the doorway a minute later.

"What?" he asked.

"I'd like to call someone."

"It's eleven o'clock at night."

"Oh." Nathan turned around—as if the blank wall behind him would give some indication that night had fallen—and then back to the correctional officer. He had a missing tooth on the right side of his mouth, and as he stood there waiting for Nathan to say more, his tongue flicked in and out of the empty cavern and made a strange, gummy sound. "Never mind."

"You can make another call in the morning."

Nathan nodded and the officer disappeared down the hall. *Eleven at night...*He shook his head. He wasn't even sure who he wanted to call. Since being detained, he learned quickly most people didn't like to pick up when an unknown number was calling. He'd tried to call Hollie once, but her mother had answered the phone and had hung up shortly after he stated who was calling. Then, he tried his own parents. They weren't dodging the calls so much as missing them. Since hearing about Nathan's circumstances, they silenced their home phone due to the sheer number of questions they didn't know how to answer that kept coming in. If Nathan was among those calls, they didn't care enough to find out. Most nights his mother spent staring at the oscillating fan above their bed and fighting back tears. His father still snored deeply through the night, but his dreams were fitful.

He thought maybe it was time to call Eliza, but that would have to wait until the morning.

He lay back down in bed and closed his eyes.

What was Eliza doing tonight? He hated himself for wondering. As his mind wandered, though, his consciousness strained further and further away. Before he knew it, his room faded away and sleep took him.

Eliza did not know Nathan thought of her as she lay down in bed that night. Her skin was still warm from her shower and her hair was still damp. Normally she would make sure it was dry before laying down; tonight, she couldn't be bothered. The sooner the world vanished the better.

For a while, she stayed corpse-like under sheet and comforter, but slowly her body grew warm, and she threw the comforter to the side. In a few minutes she started to shiver, so the comforter returned. Then, she sat up all together and stared out into the darkness, listening to the whir of the central heat.

She turned to the right and stared out her window.

Across the way, a light was on in Nathan's house.

Odd, she thought. Then, unwillingly, a voice other than her own whispered back to her, *He's still in there...*

She shivered.

Who? Who was still in there?

The light across the way then flickered out.

Eliza jumped and reached for the pillow behind her. She clung to it as she sat in the darkness, staring out at the window that just moments before had been bright. She strained her eyes to try and see through the window. The curtains were open, and she thought, for just a second that she could make out the silhouette of a person staring back at her from the window.

Then the silhouette moved.

She yelped and threw herself back onto the bed. She shook her head and stared, eyes wide, ahead of her. *No, no, no, not possible. They searched the house. They locked it after that night. The landlord came and collected all the keys.* Eliza had watched her do it.

Not all the keys, though.

She took a deep breath.

Here, keep it.

What's this?

Spare key. In case you, uh...hear anymore night terrors over here. I don't think the nightstand can take another beating.

I don't think it could take the first one.

She sat up again, and this time got up. She crossed the room and dug into the bottom drawer on her side of the dresser. She kept all her lingerie there; most of it had been untouched for months now. There, beneath her favorite Victoria Secret black bra and lace panty combo was the spare key Nathan had given her just over a month ago. She hadn't thought about it since. But now...

Over her shoulder, a light flicked back on.

She spun and saw the window lit ablaze again. Not a trick of the light, no it couldn't be. There was no silhouette in the well-lit room now, but even from across both their yards Eliza knew which room the light had turned on in.

"Tyler's," she breathed out. Her hand tightened around the key until the teeth dug into her palm. She slid it into the pocket of her pajama pants and grabbed a pair of socks from the dresser. She slipped

into them and then checked the light one last time—
still on—before heading down the stairs.

Call the cops, Eliza. Call the fucking cops.

She threw on a pair of shoes and her winter coat.
Wind lashed at her face as soon as she opened the
front door. It took more strength than usual to pull it
shut. She thought about Nathan on the other end of a
different door she'd pulled shut not long ago.

Call them—

She wasn't sure what stopped her from picking up
the phone. Call it a women's intuition, but she didn't
think the police would help with anything tonight.
They'd just get in the way. She thought about the way
they dragged Nathan down the stairs, those lonely
calls into the night as they shoved him out the door
and stuffed him in their car. *He's still there...*They
hadn't seen anyone else in the house, and they had
searched it on two separate occasions. She glanced up
at the second story window. The light was still on.
Someone was clearly still in there.

What if they got out?

What if they were armed?

She fingered the key as she trudged across her
lawn and circled up to Nathan's drive. Once there, she
jammed it into the lock and hoped—*Please, dear God,
please!*—that it wouldn't turn. Surely the landlord
changed the lock after Nathan left.

The lock clicked to the right and she felt the door
give under her hand.

She braced one hand against the door while the
other turned the knob, and slowly she pushed the
door open.

"Hello?"

Inside, a pitch darkness had taken over the foyer and living room. The curtains were drawn in the front and the back to make sure nobody could glance inside. When Eliza clicked the door shut behind her, everything in her line of sight vanished. The overwhelming scent of bleach rammed through her, and she bit down a nasty cough. She muzzled herself with the sleeve of her coat and coughed once…twice into it. *Too loud,* she thought. Still too damn loud. The noise echoed through the dark room and bounced back to her.

Nothing stirred around her.

Her breath tight, she reached out for the main light switch. As her fingers grazed the switch, she thought otherwise. *No lights.* They could be watching from across the street. If they caught even a sliver of light through the window, the neighbors would be making calls.

Instead, she stood with her back to the front door and waited for her eyes to adjust to the darkness. Slowly, shapes grew into perspective. The curving banister was the first distinguishable item, and she reached for it as soon as she could see. She planted her foot on the first stair and, knees suddenly like jelly, thought about turning right around. Had she taken a moment to think what she was doing—invading another person's house all because she thought she saw another person, who, mind you, she did consider could be dangerous, or insane, or insanely dangerous —she might've turned around. But Eliza didn't let that happen. Her other foot fell forward onto the second stair, then she lifted her first toward the third. All the while she dragged herself up by the banister. In so many ways it was all that kept her upright.

Then she stopped.

She heard something moving upstairs.

In the dark she stood and listened. The soft, subtle creak of footsteps hit her ears. They felt far away, more underwater—possibly behind one of the doors.

"Hello?" She clapped a hand across her mouth then. What was she thinking?

The footsteps stopped.

Turn back, a voice screamed at her. *Go home!*

Her feet carried her forward anyway. She thought about Nathan's last words to her, while he'd been crying and banging against the door, before he'd gone still and silent and given up hope. *He's still in here...*

Who was?

"Hello?"

Her own voice echoed back to her, but no other voice accompanied it. She thought about the silhouette in the window. It had been staring directly at her, beckoning her forward. It wanted her to keep coming. *Turn around!* She didn't. Maybe by then she couldn't. She landed at the top of the stairs and her body practically fell forward. She used the banister to heave herself upright again. When she did, she faced the darkened hallway up ahead and almost fell back down the stairs.

At the end of the hall, a shadow shifted.

Fuck! She bit back a scream as terror laced up her body. Her arm went stiff and her hand coiled hard around the banister. She squinted into the darkness but didn't see anything else moving. The second story was perfectly still.

Too still.

Tyler came to mind and her breath halted for a second. This was the place he was shot. Was it possible in some capacity...*he* was still here. The image came to mind clearly. Nathan, dragged away from his son. Nathan, whose mind was no longer sound or seeing straight. Nathan, who had only ever wanted to protect Tyler and keep him near. Nathan who...who...

He's still in there.

But no. No, he had known Tyler wasn't in there. Besides, there was fear in his voice as he called out, not agony. Whoever he was talking about, it wasn't the six-year-old boy whose life he'd taken.

Slowly, Eliza lurched herself another step forward. She looked over her shoulder once as she let go of the safety net of the banister, and struggled down the hallway. The open air was somehow more terrifying than it had been moments prior. It was the same sort of logic a child used when they thought, *If the blanket covers all of me, then the monster can't get me, right?* She felt childish as she stood there, unable to move for a moment without the banister to guide her. Then, she stumbled forward again, found the wall to her right, and grazed her open palm against it.

The wall kept her going as she passed Nathan's bedroom door. It was shut and probably locked. The stark whiteness of the painted wood almost glowed in the darkness. Eliza stopped in front of it and tried to turn one of the handles. Definitely locked. Something in her tense heart eased knowing there was one less place for something to hide. The door would be locked from the outside. Whatever she had seen from the window wasn't in there now.

Down the hall, Tyler's door hung ajar.

She stopped short of reaching it. The light was off again in the room, the homing signal dead for the night. She didn't shut her eyes, but she took a deep breath, then another, and another. Somewhere along the way the breaths stopped being deep and started becoming regular. She choked down lungfuls of stale air that slowly started to smell, and taste, like something it shouldn't. Nausea wrinkled across her stomach.

Impossible. She remembered the bleach blast as she first walked in. Everything had been cleaned up. There was no lingering smell here anymore.

And yet.

The faint aroma of rotting flesh and fecal matter clung to the open door. It clawed its way out and twisted through Eliza's lungs.

Now it was time to call the cops, wasn't it? Let them know they had combed every room but there was a shadow in the window. Tell them the bleach didn't wash everything away.

Have to find more. I'll tell them then.

But of course, she knew she wouldn't tell them. To tell the authorities was to welcome questions she wasn't ready to answer, starting with the loudest, more surefire question of them all. *Why did you go back in there?*

Why, Dear, it's because my husband was away and I couldn't sleep and, well I thought I saw someone and... and...and, well...

Because he was still in there.

She reached an arm out for the open door. Her hand connected with it, and she almost screamed from how cold the wood felt. Icy cold. The kind that felt almost hot to touch before your mind had time to react to the shock of what it was feeling, and then the freezing sank in. She lifted her hand then. It was bright red along her palm and the underbelly of each of her fingers. She lowered her palm to her side and turned into the bedroom.

The last time she had seen this room properly, she

had been rushing in after hearing Nathan scream out into the night. He stood in the center with a baseball bat and for a moment she had worried about waking him up. You weren't supposed to wake a sleepwalker. Then again, he'd been lugging around a baseball bat, and he'd been ready to swing. Waking him had been the only logical option.

Tonight, the room looked vastly different. It had been scraped of remnants of Tyler or Nathan's time there. The bed was stripped, the nightstand drawer hung ajar at a slant, any toys or clothing scattered across the carpet were now gone. Forensics teams had taken the memories out of the room and left it as a clean slate. The bed frame, the nightstand, and a small mirror that Nathan probably bought for fifteen bucks from Target were all that remained. Those would be removed by the landlord before she could start showing the house.

Then her eyes fell on the closet. The door was shut.

She thought about Nathan's night terror. The closet had been slightly ajar then, hadn't it? He'd been facing it before her voice had him turn around. He'd been armed with a baseball bat and ready to swing.

She never did ask him what exactly he thought he'd been fending off.

Eliza took a step toward the closet door.

Her fear all but doubled, though she wasn't sure why. Her heartbeat grew erratic, her forehead was clammy. The hairs on the back of her neck spiked up like a fresh breeze had just billowed behind her. The window was locked though. There was no fresh breeze or any breeze at all. She swatted her neck. It suddenly itched. *It's just a closet*, she told herself. The closer she got, though, the more uncertain she became. Plenty of things hid in closets. Kids were scared of them much longer than other, more logical fears. People hid in closets, animals, secret paths to unknown rooms in old houses...How old was Nathan's house? The floor creaked as she crossed it. One time he had mentioned old hardwood trapped under all this carpet. That had to mean it was old, right? What if someone lived in the walls, slinking through this closet each night while Nathan—and Tyler—slept.

Eliza had to know.

Nathan had known. He'd known something was wrong.

He's still in here...

It occurred to her for the first time since that night: what if Nathan hadn't been aiming at Tyler? What if the gun was pointed at someone else, but Tyler had gotten in the way? Her hand found the doorknob. As it did, she saw a shadow pass in the gap between the carpet and door. She released the handle, jumped back. *Go home,* she thought. *I should go home.* She tilted her head and bent over slightly to try and get a better look at the space she'd seen the shadow. As she did, she swore she heard a low, ragged breath escape from the other end of the closet. Someone was in there. She stood straight and grabbed for the doorknob again. *No, I have to—*

She pulled the closet door open.

He woke suddenly in the dead of night. Sweat bled from a crease in his forehead and his eyelids were heavy, but alert. He laid there, eyes open and looking straight up at the top bunk.

What was that?

He had awoken to a sound like fingernails scratching against hardwood. As far as he was aware, nothing in the room was made of real wood. Everything was either metal, plastic made to look like metal, or plastic that wasn't disguised as anything but what it was.

The sound of running water hit his ears.

He craned his neck toward the toilet. The faucet at the top of it had suddenly turned on. A slow trickle of steady water drained into the basin below. In the otherwise silent holding cell, Nathan could make out the sound of it swirling down the drain and running through the pipes over him. For an instant the whole room seemed to quell with the sound of sloshing water.

He sat up. A dim light came from the hall outside his cell. The ghostly echo of workman's boots grew faint in the distance as the night guard paced away from Nathan's room. The hallway light seemed almost to flicker the longer Nathan sat in his bed. He turned away from the light and got up to shut the water off. When had he turned it on? *Faulty pipes,* he figured as he twisted the faucet and the water clogged up. He looked up then and met his own reflection's eyes in the security mirror above the sink. As he did, he felt a breeze whisper along the back of his neck.

Nathan shivered.

There was nowhere for a breeze to come in from.

What time is it? He absentmindedly turned the water back on and then off again.

When he looked up again, he noticed something shift behind his reflection. Shadows spidered out from behind his bed, and whether it was due to the flickering hall light or something else, one of those shadows seemed to move independently of the others.

It stretched along the wall and wrapped around the far corner of the room. There, it sat and hid among the other shadows. Nathan trained his vision on it but didn't turn around. His grip tightened on the sides of the sink.

Who's there? he thought. When he tried to call out, his lips did not move. He thought he heard a soft chuckle in reply but couldn't be sure. He sucked in a deep, hollow breath and shook his head. There was nothing there. The shadows remained put, still once again.

Then, the same dark spot as before started to wriggle free of the others. He watched it bubble out from the cement wall and twist its way into the third dimension.

Impossible.

Another shadow, this one double the size of the first, also popped out from the rest of the wall. Slowly, the two shadows morphed into two spindly arms— one short...and one long. The wide brim of a hat poked out from the middle of them, and the Lop-Sided man opened his blazing, yellow eyes.

Nathan tried to move as the shadow grew closer, but his body refused to comply. "Help." This time his lips did part, though his voice came out chalky, whispered. "Help me." He no longer heard the officer's footsteps down the hall. Where had he vanished to? "Hello?" he called again. His voice was growing desperate, his throat tight. A shortness of breath overtook him and his head started spinning. He tried to shut his eyes, but couldn't keep them closed. The shadow man behind him hunched forward off the wall and lunged in his direction. Nathan stood there and watched. He tried not to think of Tyler.

A losing battle, always a losing battle.

This was a fucking losing battle from the start.

From the start—

From the—

The Lop-Sided man reached his longer arm forward and Nathan felt the spidery tingle of fingers creep across the nape of his neck.

This started too long ago. He thought about open curtains and a wife who refused to cry, even though her body screamed and shattered. This had started then, in an old house, with a younger him. *You knew me then. You saw me.* Saw him in a crowded arena, running through crowds wearing masks and throwing bloody bottles his way. *How long have you been here... how long have you followed?*

Finish it, he thought. *Finish it now.*

His breathing was ragged. His eyes darted to either side. *Finish it.* There was nowhere he could run. The cell was seven feet by eight feet with bars blocking any path to safety. *Finish it. Finish it*—

"Now!"

The fingers bit into Nathan's neck and squeezed his windpipe shut. One nail bit into his throat and Nathan felt it push through the fleshy cartilage surrounding his trachea. He sputtered out a final breath as the nail dug deeper, then yanked free with a splatter of warm blood slashed across the mirror. Nathan keeled forward but the hand wrapped around the back of his neck pulled him upright. Fire burned up his esophagus as he struggled for breath. His head was yanked to the side, and Nathan stared ahead into the mirror as the Lop-Sided man's glowing, golden eyes seared into him. The last thing he'd see. The last thing he'd—

His chest heaved once...twice...desperate for air as blood poured from the hole in his throat. He was drowning from the inside out, the world slowly fading around him. As the world went dark, he saw a piece of the shadow's head split in two, and a wide, toothy grin glistened in the dying light.

Then, Nathan Cooley saw no more.

Eliza braced herself as it swung open, but when the door softly knocked against the wall, Eliza Shepherd saw nothing. The shelves were lined with blankets and kid clothes, plus a couple stuffed animals and action figures, too. The landlord hadn't cleared this place out yet either. In so many ways it was the only part of the room that even looked lived in. She reached out and moved some of the hanging shirts aside, but there was nothing on the back wall of the closet. She pushed against it to make sure, but the wall didn't budge. Tension eased in her. No hidden door at the back of the closet. She scanned down.

There was something on the floor.

She bent forward for the single piece of paper in the center of the closet. On it was a drawing. It was done entirely in what looked like black ink and had a sketch-like quality to it; the lines were jagged, and the shading was harsh. Somewhere in it though, Eliza made out the room she was standing in. One wall had a giant window, the other a bed sat against. The bed was unkempt, messy. The middle of the room was stained dark. She looked back and saw no similar stain. In the drawing, the closet door was shut, but something dark and inky spilled out from the bottom of it. It looked almost similar to the small puddle in the middle of the room.

She looked up, and as she did, she felt the whisk of

the closet door slamming against her body. Eliza squealed as it hit against her, then she turned. She wasn't far enough into the closet for it to slam shut. She stepped out of the closet, then craned her neck around to see what had tried to close the door on her.

The other side of the closet door was empty. There was nothing there.

She looked down at the picture in her hand, then again at the empty closet.

Droooooopppp it, a voice whispered from somewhere behind her.

She shivered and the drawing fell from between her fingers. As it floated down and landed back in the very same spot it had been in last, Eliza turned on her heels and ran. She sprinted down the stairs, the distinct feeling that someone was right behind her following her all the way down and out the front door. She didn't care that the door was still unlocked as she ran across the lawn. There wasn't time to change that. She looked over her shoulder only once as she reached her own front door. She had left it unlocked and easily swung the door open, then slammed it shut behind her.

Only then did she let out a shaky, rattling breath.

She still felt the closet door jamming into her back. Something had pushed it. Something had...

He's still in there...

She grabbed for her phone that still sat on the couch. There were no messages from Ethan after all. She dropped the phone again. She should call the police, tell them what happened. Someone was in that house. Some*thing* was still stalking through it.

He's still in there...

But no. She couldn't call them. They wouldn't know what to do. And another search would result in nothing new. They combed through that house twice. *Twice!* If something was still in there, they would've found it.

Eliza slumped onto the couch and let her head fall into her hands. Her shoulders quivered, but she did not cry. She wasn't sure what hour it was now, but she knew she had to go to bed. Fall asleep. Leave tonight behind. She stood from the couch so quickly she went suddenly lightheaded.

Eliiizzzaaaaa...

The voice came from somewhere behind her. She peered over her shoulder, but the wall behind her was blank. She stared at it a moment longer, then turned again to face forward. She shook her head. There was nothing there.

And yet.

She knew what she had heard.

The walk up the stairs and to her lonely bedroom took longer than it should have that night. When she got there, she checked once more to see if the light was still on in Nathan's house.

The window was dark.

Somehow, that convinced her that tonight's horrors were done. She stripped off her jacket and shoes —she would move them back to the front door tomorrow morning once the sun came up again—and crawled into bed. The comforter felt heavy and warm overtop her, and she shivered not from the cold but from the sudden relief of its cover. *Go to sleep,* she thought. *Just go to sleep.*

Only, her mind still raced as she lay there. She thought of the picture she'd found in the closet. Who had left it there? Who had drawn it? She turned again out the window and stared out at Nathan's dark house.

If there was a silhouette among the darkness, she couldn't tell.

Briefly, Eliza Shepherd shut her eyes.

She opened them again when she heard a familiar whisper, *Eliiizzzaaaaa…*

She sat up. "Who's there?"

The darkness didn't answer back. She sat there, comforter across her stomach and pillow digging into her back, for a few moments longer. Then, satisfied that she had imagined the whisper, she laid back down. It took a while longer for sleep to claim her, but like every nightmare that went bump in the night, the revolving terror could only last so long. Soon, her eyelids grew heavy and the room around her started to fade.

Eliza Shepherd—whose maiden name had been Williams, she pondered as she fell asleep, wondering if maybe she would like to use it again sometime soon —didn't dream that night after falling asleep.

And for that she was thankful.

16

" And you didn't hear anything else?"

It was late the next morning. The little hand was just passing ten on the clock above private investigator Ryan Leery's head. Leery sat across from Correctional Officer Markie in the warden's private office. Markie had discovered the inmate's body crumpled on the floor next to his toilet, his neck jutting out at an awkward angle, broken somehow in the night, at six that morning, and called in for backup immediately. There were suspicions of foul play, though Leery could not see how.

"Nada," Markie said, and let out a yawn.

Last night had been long. The night shift always was. Now, he kept glancing precariously at the clock ticking away over Leery's head, and wondering when he'd be able to get the hell outta Wayne County and tuck himself in for a long slumber. He always slept well after night shifts. Today he suspected would rival even his greatest post-shift sleeping spells.

"Zilch." A cigarette dangled loosely from between his lips.

"And you suspect foul play as well."

"Didn't say that," said Markie. "Just said he didn't do it on his own."

"And how come?"

"I dunno. Just don't seem right."

"Yes, well—"

"He hadn't had the trial yet. They don't do all that so quickly here."

"Yes, well it's my understanding he had been talking to a lawyer and the date was set."

"Sure."

"And as it grew closer perhaps the guilt maybe wore at him and...and...well..."

Leery trailed off and Markie leaned forward. There was a table between them with an ash tray and a pile of magazines strewn across it. The officer tipped his cigarette into the tray and then replaced it between his lips.

"Far as I'm concerned...no man's guilty enough to wake in the middle o' the night and slam his neck against the rim of a toilet hard 'nough to break bone."

Leery swallowed. "They said you found a note?"

Markie dropped the rest of his cigarette into the tray. He didn't bother to put it out, and a thin strand of twirling smoke rose between the PI and the correctional officer.

"Note? Nah. Found this though." He reached behind him for a paper and handed it over to Leery.

"What's this?"

"A drawing," said the warden. "Found it under his bed." He leaned across the table and plucked his cigarette from the ash tray. "What do you make of that?"

"It's...it's scribbles."

"Scribbles, sure. Sure, I can see that. I can also see a bed. And a toilet with a mirror over it. Do you see an inmate though?"

"N-no I...I don't."

What both men saw was a sketchy replica of the inmate's cell on the day he was brought to it. Same set of bunked beds, same desk with the chair tucked in, same bathroom nook. In the center of the drawn room stood a man. He had one regular sized arm and one long one, and he wore a wide brimmed hat that shrouded his face in darkness.

Leery looked up and met Markie's eyes.

"This doesn't point to foul play," Leery said.

But the officer split his mouth into a thin smile. "Oh sure it does," he said. "There's more than one kind of foul play. Far as I'm concerned that inmate wasn't alone in that cell, and that's as foul as the playin' can get."

"I-I would like to take this back to the office. Have it examined for fingerprints. Maybe we can see if—"

"Burn it when you're done."

Leery stopped. "Pardon?"

"Burn it."

"Burn—Sir you better start making sense."

"I'm making perfect sense. That picture...it don't feel right," Markie said. "Don't it?"

Leery stared back down at the image. The shadowy man's hat seemed tipped slightly up now. He could make out more of the man's jaw and the slightest corner of an eyeball. He squinted at that corner. "Where'd he get yellow ink?"

The officer stood up. "Same place he got the first pen and the piece of paper." Leery eyed him curiously. "He didn't."

He smushed his cigarette into the ash tray then and a final cloud of smoke simmered up. As he walked toward the door and propped it up, Leery sat with the image awhile longer. *That inmate wasn't alone in that* *cell...and that's as foul as it gets...*He turned to Markie again. The officer was standing in the open doorway now. "We done here?" he asked.

"I—yes, I suppose we are," said Leery. He stood then and followed Markie out. The heavy door swung shut behind them. "Thank you."

"'Course."

Both men shared a long glance, then looked down at the drawing between them. "And you're sure nobody gave him a pen and paper?"

"He never asked for any," said Markie.

Leery looked down at the drawing again, then extended his arm and held it out for Markie. "I won't be needing this," he said. His fingertips were frigid where they touched the paper, and as soon as Markie snatched it away, warmth spread through them again.

"Figured," said Markie. Another officer was crossing by them, and Markie nudged his shoulder. "Hey, Sammy. Send this one to the shredder." He passed off the drawing and the other officer nodded and headed off back the way he'd come.

Markie turned back to Ryan Leery. "I'll walk ya out," he said.

"Thank you."

The correctional officer nodded and led the two of them down the main hall. When they opened the doors into the main reception area with its round front desk that was blocked off with plexiglass, he saw the sunlight glowing the way it only did when bouncing off a fresh snowfall. Temperatures had dropped further in the night and were expected to keep falling until Christmas. The thought of having a nice, hot shower when he got home crossed Markie's mind. He held the door open for Leery when they reached it and waved him off. "Have a nice day," he said.

"You do the same."

Then, before the door shut between them, Markie noticed Leery glance again at the hand that'd been holding the drawing. He let out a little huff of air.

"Feels wrong, don't it?"

Leery looked up and took a deep breath. "It's just the cold," he told him.

"Right. And that'll fade." In the distance, Markie thought he heard the humming sound of a paper shredder. "It always does."

Leery nodded and the two men parted ways with a final wave. Markie went to clock out; Leery went to start his car. Neither man thought again about the drawing they'd held momentarily between them, or why the crisp piece of paper had felt like a sheet of solid ice whenever touched. Some things were better not to dwell on for too long.

Stephanie Hill sat at the front desk when Markie went behind it to use the spare computer to clock out. She was one of the part-timers who worked behind the front desk. Markie was partial to Stephanie's nighttime counterpart, Rebecca, but he liked Stephanie well enough. Today she was reading a battered paperback that she set aside when he walked up.

"He's finally gone?" she asked.

"Hmm? Yeah, he's gone."

"Did he find anything?"

"No. What was he s'posed to find?"

"I dunno. Some of the guys were talking about maybe someone else sneaking into the room with him or something. I thought it might be interesting."

Markie glanced at the cover of her book. A

skeleton was holding up a pocket watch and staring forward through empty eye sockets.

"Lay off the creepers books before the next shift," Markie joked.

Stephanie laughed and pushed her glasses up the bridge of her nose. She was a right beauty from behind them, but the wire frames made her look about ten years older than Markie reckoned she was, and they cut off her wide, blue eyes. "So no foul play."

"Is that what I said?"

Her smile faltered. The space between them went suddenly cold. "Is it?"

Markie shrugged and finished typing in his hours. He stood up and circled the desk again. "A man 'n his thoughts can sometimes be plenty foul enough." Then, he smacked his hand against the front of the desk and Stephanie jumped. "You work tomorrow?"

"Same as always," she said.

"Good, good. Might catch ya then."

"Alrighty. See you."

She watched the door swing shut behind him, and shortly after the room returned to its former quiet state. She reached for her book again but thought better of it. Something in the back of her mind told her to leave it there. *A man 'n his thoughts can be plenty foul enough...*

Cold ran down the back of Stephanie Hill's neck.

She did not pick her paperback up again for the rest of her shift. The room was suddenly too cold, the bitter kind of cold that cut deep inside bone and wriggled its way into the bloodstream. It was all she could think about as she wrapped her cardigan tighter around her body and glanced at the clock on her computer. *Ten o' nine.* The day was still just getting started, but she was suddenly very ready for it to end. Sitting there in the lonely reception area of the Wayne County jail, Stephanie Hill thought again and again about what Markie had told her before walking out. She pushed her novel further away from her, and sunk deeper into her seat.

Overhead the clock ticked...and ticked...and ticked...and there was nothing left to do but wait for the day to die.

ACKNOWLEDGMENTS

Even though I've been writing for as long as I can remember, no novel (even a short one) gets told alone. And I believe a few thanks are in order.

First, this novel wouldn't be possible without the help of Mark Becker's editing hand. He couldn't fix all the rambling, but he certainly made it better. Thank you Ed Wishewsky for the beautiful cover art, and my partner Josh Carter for designing the cover itself, adding the font, and making sure it shined. Thank you, babe, for also being the first person to read every story I write and always encouraging me to keep going. Without you this story truly would not have been finished as fast as it was. Thank you to the friends who pushed me, to my family who supported me, and to everyone who for the last twenty some odd years has heard me mouthing off that "one day I'll do it, one day I'll be an author."

Here's your proof. Let it be the first of many.

ABOUT THE AUTHOR

Jacob Elliott has been writing stories for as long as he can remember. He taught himself to type at the age of five, and started writing "novels" for his family to "publish" (aka take to the printer and bind in a spiral notebook) shortly after. In high school he founded the Young Writer's League and then went on to major in Creative Writing in college. It wasn't until 2020 that he found a love of horror novels and quickly amassed a collection. The Lop-Sided Man is his first published novel and fulfills a lifetime goal to see his work in print. Currently, he lives in Detroit, Michigan where he dotes over his two cats and budding plant collection like his life depends on it. When he isn't writing... or reading...or daydreaming about his next project, you can find him talking through reality tv shows with friends or playing Nintendo video games. For now, he is working hard on his next project and cannot wait for you to read more.

For writing and life updates, follow him on Instagram @jacob_elliott_books.

For questions and inquiries, email him directly at authorjacobelliott@gmail.com.